CITY OF DEATH

CONNOR WHITELEY

No part of this book may be reproduced in any form or by any electronic or mechanical means. Including information storage, and retrieval systems, without written permission from the author except for the use of brief quotations in a book review.

This book is NOT legal, professional, medical, financial or any type of official advice.

Any questions about the book, rights licensing, or to contact the author, please email connorwhiteley@connorwhiteley.net

Copyright © 2021 CONNOR WHITELEY

All rights reserved.

DEDICATION
Thank you to all my readers without you I couldn't do what I love.

CHAPTER 1

Everyone will die. But whether or not I will kill you is down to you.

Breathing in the smoke filled air, I pressed my body against the cold wood of a bakery as I scout out my next location.

I always like to be near a bakery because sometimes you can easily steal something and dash off into the distance. Granted I normally give the stolen good to a starving child but I still love stealing.

Wearing my thick black leather armour and black cloak, I made sure my smooth face was covered up. I was not going to be recognised here, especially with all those crazy bounty hunters who want my head.

Looking forward, my eyes narrowed on the busy street full of busy common people walking past in their smelly clothes. I wish some of these people would take a bath, but I guess they aren't, and that's why I do what I do.

I want to help people.

As I looked past the crowd in the busy dirty street, I turned my attention to the massive solid grey stone wall ahead in between two bigger towers. I smiled and placed my hands on the hilt of my two long black swords.

The sounds of the people chatting and talking filled my ears as I focused on the wall ahead. I needed to focus and analyse my target, a lot of people would have said how I analyse buildings and people is flat out weird. I prefer to think of it as making sure I stay alive.

Two entrance points by ladders about twenty metres away. A large crowd in my way. Definitely not my favourite conditions to get to a target but not my worse and these people in the street were hardly enemies.

Stretching my neck a little, my eyes narrowed on the grey armoured guards on the wall. Six guards, that should be easy enough to kill but I needed to do it quickly.

Then I smiled as I looked at what my real target was, from where I was standing I couldn't see it perfectly clear but it was enough.

Looking at the large brown crates with wooden bars across the top, my smile didn't stop as I imagined the birds inside. I needed only one bird but that was risky.

Making sure my hood was up, I walked into the street carefully, trying to blend into the crowd (and trying not to gag on the body odour of these commoners!). In the back of my mind, I knew I had to succeed here or many great people would die.

As I passed through the crowd towards the massive grey wall, I couldn't believe I was doing this in all honesty. For my entire life I have been a cold, calculating assassin. Killing for a paycheck and loving every moment of it. But damn that Rebellion with their kind words, warm hearts and their cause. They hooked me in tightly so when I learnt on my last mission that stupid, tyrannical Overlord had sent an army to kill them.

I sadly grew a damn conscience.

So I rode here, wrote a warning note and now I want to, no have to attach this to a bird and release it. The Rebellion has to get my note, they have to live.

Another breath of horrible sweat made me cough, and oddly enough it reminded me of the juicy salt bacon breakfast my mother use to make.

As I got closer to the wall, I gripped the hilts of my swords as I noticed two grey armoured guards next to the ladder. I saw two other guards take the other ladder away. I was not impressed!

The two guards started to look at me, under my hood I started to wonder what to do to them. Should I kill them quickly? Stab them in the liver and let them bleed out slowly?

I rolled my eyes as I realised because I had to save my friends and all the other Rebels, I sadly didn't have time to play with my prey.

I walked up to them.

The Guards frowned.
Reaching for their swords.
I whipped out mine.
Slashing their throats.
Someone shouted.
I charged up the wooden ladder.
A Guard charged at me.
I jumped into the air.
Kicking him in the head.
He fell off the wall.
His corpse smashed below.
Another two Guards attacked.
I looked at the crates.
I needed to move.
The Guards swung.
I dodged.
Leaping back up.
Thrusting my swords into their heads.
I charged to the crates.
Got out my note.
An arrow hit the ground.
I spun.
Two Guards fired.
I grabbed the arrows.
Snapping them.
The Guards stopped.
I charged.
Jumping into the air.
Another Guard fired.
I caught the arrow.

Thrusting it in their head.
The arrow exploded out the back.
Blood gushed out.
I landed on the Guard.
Wrapping my legs around her neck.
I swung my body weight.
She fell.
Slamming onto the ground.
I snapped her neck.
One more Guard.
I jumped up.
The air moved.
I ducked.
A blade rushed past.
I slammed my fists into his face.
He whacked me.
He swung his sword.
I jumped.
Leaping over the sword.
I swung my swords.
Slicing off his hands.
He screamed.
I silenced him.
I smashed his skull in.
Common people stared at me.
I had to act.
I rushed to the crates.
Opening them.
I heard more Guards coming.
Grabbing a little grey bird.

Attaching my note.
I threw it into the air.
It flew.
Arrows flew through the air.
The enemy were attacking.
I looked at the crate.
There were more birds.
I had to protect my friends.
I launched all the birds.
Twenty birds flew into the air.
Arrows roared through them.
Birds were slaughtered.

As I watched the little corpses fall to the ground, I smiled as I watched the bird with my note fly off far, far into the distance.

Maybe my friends would be safe and maybe my warning would be enough, but I had to make sure they were safe, and for that I needed allies.

CHAPTER 2

Commander Coleman stared out over his amazing valley and mountain range that surrounded his Rebel stronghold. He loved it here, he loved everything about it.

Coleman wasn't exactly sure what his favourite part was but he sure loved how the sharp dagger-like black mountains in the distance provided some protection for his stronghold.

Feeling the cold, hard rock under his feet, Coleman knew he needed to be prepared. He couldn't place the feeling, everyone else thought he was mad, but he felt like something was coming.

Something to end them all.

Coleman checked report after report about the horrific activities of the Overlord and all his puppet Kings. There was nothing in the reports. Coleman still had that nagging feeling.

Smelling the fresh, crisp air of the mountain, Coleman smiled and turned his attention to admiring the stunning valley between the black mountains and him. It was amazing watching the little rabbits and deer run and hop and eat down there on the lust green ground.

Coleman wished his life was that simple but as he turned around and looked down from his watch post. He smiled for a different reason as he remembered how he wouldn't have it any other way.

Looking down at the twisting, turning rocky mountain that the Rebellion called home, Coleman felt a wave of pride wash over him. He was proud and he loved this mountain, it was where Coleman could change things and help people live better lives.

That's what he loved.

Coleman had picked every man and woman in this base, he had trained them and from here Coleman loved how he was trying to change the fate of the Kingdom.

Listening to the gentle howl of the cold wind, he remembered a woman once asking him why he bothered fighting the Overlord and why doesn't he just stay in the mountain and live in peace.

Sometimes Coleman laughed or smiled at that memory but it was so important. It was important that Coleman remembered why he did this. He didn't do it because he wanted to rule and have subjects.

Coleman wanted people to be free and choose how they lived their lives. Instead of being forced down a particular path depending on which City the person lived in.

He shuddered as he remembered where he lived before he formed the Rebellion. Coleman hated how the City of Pleasure in the North made him train for hours each day to make sure he had the correct body for his purpose in life.

Even now Coleman's hands formed fists as he remembered how everyone common man and woman in the City of Pleasure was destined to become a sex object.

That's why he did what he did. No one, absolutely no one should have to do that.

Turning back to staring out over the valley and the mountains beyond, Coleman tried to think about what to do. He couldn't do anything military related because he only had a hunch and Coleman could never, ever risk the lives of his friends without it meaning something.

After a few moments of thinking and wondering about how to prepare for this invisible threat that was coming, Coleman's stomach twisted into a tight knot.

A small part of Coleman couldn't get that beautiful, mysterious assassin out of his head. He knew it was silly, after all she was a dangerous assassin who only killed because he paid her.

But he loved that smooth, pale face and that long brown hair. He loved how confident she was, but Coleman tried to push those thoughts away as he knew they were fantasies. He couldn't act on them and even if he did, he sadly knew he would be putting the cause at risk.

As Coleman turned and started to walk away (hoping he could form a plan in his office), he heard a strange shrieking, and he smiled as he saw a little green bird land on his shoulder.

It shrieked. Coleman forgot how loud and annoying delivery birds were.

Then he cocked his head as he noticed a small thin piece of parchment on the bird. Taking it off, Coleman rolled his eyes and his stomach relaxed a little as he saw the name on it.

The Assassin.

Coleman felt his cheeks turn rosy at the idea of his Assassin writing to him and maybe it was a love letter. Coleman laughed at that idea, of course it wasn't.

Opening the parchment, Coleman's eyes narrowed as he realised this was not a love letter in the slightest. He was right. Something was very, very wrong.

Coleman ran down the mountain. "Call the War Council!"

CHAPTER 3

Rain lashed and slashed at me as I rode along the long twisting dirt road towards my next target. I needed to see an old friend, a warlord in fact.

As I felt my beautiful (stolen) brown horse moan and trod along, I took a moment to relax a little and consider my next moves, but the air did have a wonderful crispiness to it and a hint of cedarwood and dry pine.

Looking ahead, my eyes narrowed as I saw a large bend in the dirt road and the fact that the road was lined with thick dense trees didn't help the matter. The last thing I wanted was to be ambushed.

Just in case I placed a hand on the hilt of my long sword, I was going to be prepared. I raised the black hood of my long black trench coat and cloak to be on the safe side.

If there was an ambush I didn't want these stupid ambushers to recognise me and see a payday riding towards them!

Listening to the awful singing of birds and the rustling of the leaves in the gentle cool wind, I remembered the first time I met Lord Baron Huin, it was on a mission and I had been sent to slaughter his wife for a client (not the Rebellion) and well... he was hardly impressed. So we fought, I sliced off his hand and I did my mission.

It took another two years for us to meet again and become friends. It turned out I did him a favour. It's strange how these things work out, but that's part of my job as a female assassin, I kill for the money and sometimes (damn the Rebellion) I kill for a good cause.

Even now, I still can't believe what I'm doing, if it was anyone else I would have learnt they were in trouble, sent the note and be done with it. There are plenty of people who would hire me and pay me well to kill for them.

And if I was really, really pushed for work and money (Like that would ever happen!), I suppose I could always ask the Overlord for work and explain I only killed all his people because it was my job. And if he refused, well, I would have to kill him.

The birds started to fall silent.

But that Rebellion and their goody tooshie cause, it definitely makes you a fan so I have to ride on and I have to get my old friend to help us.

My stomach tightened as I thought about my note not getting to the Rebellion, and that's another reason I have to get my old friend to help us. If his war party, or whatever he calls them these days, can reinforce the Rebellion, then there's an extremely slim chance we would win.

And maybe, just maybe I'll be able to see that hot Commander Coleman again. I smiled as I remembered that amazing, attractive man with his large muscles, smooth square face and a strong jawline. Maybe I was doing all this to save him, and him alone. I would like to think not but you never know.

A twig snapped.

As I got closer to the bend in the road, I drew out my sword just in case. The air felt off here. Like it had been disturbed.

I heard something step out of the trees behind me. As I turned I stayed calm, there was no point getting angry here.

Cocking my head, I had no idea what I was looking at as I stared at a tall man cloaked in darkness and black cloaks. Almost like he was half man, half shadow. It didn't make sense, even his face was shrouded in darkness.

He drew out his sword. I frowned. It sounded like the blade was quietly screaming.

I hopped off my horse. Two more shadowy people stepped out behind me. I was surrounded.

"I know a pretti bag of goldie for me and ya head," the first shadowy man said, his vice dark, twisted but had a weird angelic edge to it.

"Sorry to disappoint you!" I shouted.

I whipped out my other sword.
I charged.
Flying through the air.
My swords swung.
The shadow man swung.
Our swords clashed.
Locking our swords together.
Lightning shot out of his.
Annihilating a tree.
Other trees burned.
The other men charged.
I kicked the shadow man.
He unlocked our swords.
I swung.
Slashing his shadowy cheek.
Nothing happened.
The air moved.
I raised my swords.
Meeting three blades.
I jumped into the air.
Kicking them.
Icy coldness shot into me.
My feet turned numb.
I wasn't kicking them again.
I turned to run.
I couldn't run properly.
The shadow men charged.
I tried to hop away.
I couldn't.
The men swung.

I rolled forward.

Dodging the attacks.

I tried to stand up.

I couldn't.

My feet were numb.

The men rushed over.

Raising their swords.

Feeling returned to my feet.

Not enough though.

I needed more time.

Lightning buzzed from their swords.

The air smelt burned.

I swirled my swords.

The enemy jumped back.

My sword sliced one of them.

Nothing happened.

No scream.

No blood.

No nothing.

The enemy swung.

I could feel my feet.

I rolled back.

Missing the swords.

I jumped up.

Thrusting my swords into their backs.

Two corpses dropped.

The last one stared at me.

After a second or two, I realised he was pointing and gesturing me to look at the two corpses I had made.

Taking a few steps back I did, the black shadowy corpses laid there as dead as any of my other targets. There was nothing special about them.

Small amounts of lightning buzzed around the bodies and they moved.

My eyes widened in horror as I realised what these creatures were. These weren't any humans or mortals they were Hunters. Some people called them demons. Others called them warlocks.

I didn't care what they were called but they were horrific foes.

I flew forward.

Kicking them in the head.

The lightning disappeared.

The other shadowy figure screamed.

My ears bleed.

I spun.

Rushing to my horse.

I jumped on it.

I escaped.

As I rode away as fast as I could, I couldn't deny the thought of having Hunters after me, scared me more than anyone could ever know.

CHAPTER 4

Commander Coleman felt the cold black leather chair he sat in moulded to his body as he looked at the large cave office ahead of him.

Coleman smiled as he remembered how many newbies to the Rebellion had come into his office and commented on how underwhelmed they had been to see this was the amazing, grand office of the Rebellion.

As Coleman looked around at the rough domed walls of the cave and the rough grey floor of the office. Coleman understood why people weren't impressed with his office, but as he always said to them he didn't want to spend money on an office. He would rather spend the money on the starving people that were being abused and sometimes raped by the Overlord's people.

Yet there was something about his office that Coleman loved, he just couldn't place his finger on. Maybe it was the sweet smell of the sugary piney incense that was burning in the corner. Maybe it was the large brown table he sat at with a massive map of the Kingdom covered in little wooden eagles and men.

He didn't know in all honesty, Coleman just loved it. Especially as he turned his attention to the map out in front of him, there were so many wooden men on the map showing all the Overlord strongholds and the Cities the Overlord still held.

There were too few Eagles on the map. His favourite animal.

A part of him doubted this could ever work and Coleman knew he would never win against the Warlord. The only reason there were the eagles on the map was because of that beautiful Assassin.

Coleman smiled as he thought about her long black trench coat and her amazing figure. She was stunning.

A small part of him knew it was silly but he really wanted to believe she had sent the note for only him. To protect him and show in her beautiful assassin way, she was trying to protect him so she could have him later on. He knew it was silly but he hoped it was true.

The sound of the knocking on heavy wood and muttering outside of the office made Coleman rolled his eyes. As much as he loved leading the Rebellion, Coleman really didn't enjoy these meetings or so-called War Council.

"Come in," Coleman said.

The heavy wooden door opened and Coleman gave a small grin as one man and two women wandered in. All wearing thick, heavy metal armour.

Nodding his respect to the two women, Coleman admired how these two amazing sisters (Abbic and Barbic) always managed to look so stunning for these meetings with their long perfectly straight blond hair and their smooth faces.

Coleman stopped that train of thought as he remembered them on the battlefield. He knew (from personal experience) how deadly and aggressive these two were. He wasn't going to underestimate them like so many enemies did.

"Commander," the man said, his voice rough and deep but Coleman liked Captain Dragnist with his long black bead and scars covering his face from gods know how many battles.

"Me Lord, why did ya call us?" Abbic asked.

Coleman loved how smooth her voice was and wanted to laugh because it made her sound harmless.

"Thank you coming all of you. I received this note from the Assassin earlier," Coleman said, passing them the note.

Barbic cocked her head. "This Assassin is warning us of some invasion. Oh please. She is a no good trouble maker,"

Coleman's eyes narrowed. "You think she is lying?"

"Of course, dearest Coleman. She is a dirty Assassin. No good. She is a troublemaker, this is probably fake,"

"I donna know Sis, this note looks gooda to me,"

"Seriously Abbic? This Assassin says the enemy will launch themselves from the City of Death. That's rubbish. The City of Death hasn't been stepped foot in for a thousand years,"

Coleman rolled his eyes as he knew that was completely wrong. He had walked in the City a few years ago but Coleman would never, ever do it again. He felt there was a good reason why no one lived there anymore. He just might have been too scared to find out.

Dragnist frowned. "That not true and yo know it. Overlord use it mining stuff,"

Coleman nodded. "Whatever is going on with the City of Death. I am not taking any chances and I do believe the Assassin because-"

"Dearest Coleman, we all know you have a soft spot for her but she is a dangerous no good Assassin. She will kill you. The Overlord only needs to pay her enough,"

Leaning forward Coleman stared Barbic dead in the eye.

"I am in charge here. I will defend the Rebellion to the end. My question to you is what should we do about it? I would send a scout party to the City but I don't want to waste manpower,"

"Bossie and if tha Overlord is there. We don't wanna get them slaughtered,"

"No Sister we don't. I propose we get allies,"

Coleman leant back in his chair and smiled at that idea. Barbic must have seen his smile as she passed him the Assassin's note and pointed to the bottom.

"Dearest Coleman, you see here,"

Focusing on the note, Coleman looked at the little word on the bottom of the parchment it meant nothing to him. It was a single name of a town tens of miles away. It was abandoned for all Coleman knew, it wasn't important.

"So?" Coleman asked.

Barbic rolled her eyes. "This is a town twenty miles away,"

"I know but it's abandoned,"

"Na it isn't bossie. Ya old friend lives there. Ya know, Lord Baron Huin," Abbic said.

Coleman couldn't believe he was hearing that name again, it had easily been five years maybe longer. Coleman had no idea why the beautiful Assassin would be going there. But he wanted to see her and maybe Coleman could get the Lord Baron to help them.

He had to try.

"You three can control whilst I'm away. I have to see Huin," Coleman said, walking away before anyone could argue.

As he walked out the heavy wooden door, Coleman felt his stomach fill with butterflies as the idea of seeing his beautiful Assassin filled him with excitement.

He just hoped she would feel the same.

CHAPTER 5

I was hoping not to have to use my backup plan but it seems worth it now. There was a very special reason why I chose to ride across this stretch of the dirt road.

Sliding off my strong brown horse, I made sure my long black leather trench coat and cloak covered my body and face, as I felt the soft mud move under my feet.

Well, at least I hope it was mud but judging by the strong smell, I doubt it.

As I pretended to tie my horse to a wooden post, I looked around and studied the dirt street in this small town. It certainly wouldn't have been my first choice as places to hide or concoct some sort of scheme but it was okay. And to be honest, anywhere I can kill someone is okay to me.

My eyes narrowed on the large dirty muddy square surrounded by little wooden houses. They didn't seem dangerous and I doubted the Hunters would have got here before me so I should be safe for a few minutes.

Turning my attention to the crowd, I rolled my eyes as one man's mouth dropped as he looked at my *assets*. I hated men like that, maybe I should accidentally swing my blade later on.

Listening to the talk of the crowd and the high pitch laughter, my eyes were drawn to the tall women dancing in the middle of the square. I cocked my head as I realised there wasn't any music or anything to dance to. Why were they dancing?

I checked again if my hood was covering most of my face and when I knew it was, I slowly walked through the square. Smelling the oddly perfumed air from the women I passed and the disgusting hints of alcohol I got from the men I passed.

As much as I hated walking through the crowd that was getting increasingly busy as the dancing continued, I needed to wait until the Hunters got here to fight back. I had a feeling they were tracking me somehow.

I just needed to test it.

In the back of my mind, I could feel myself wanting to scream out for help and panic at the idea of the Hunters after me. In all my years of being an assassin, I had heard rumours of these supernatural killers that massacred people and entire Cities for the Overlord. But I never believed them.

I'm not exactly sure why, but I think it's because after the Overlord annihilated the Temple of

Assassins and killed all my friends and mentors. There are just so few assassins anymore.

I smiled at the idea of being the last of a dying breed and maybe I was. Despite popular belief, assassins aren't typical commoners trained to kill.

My stomach twisted at the memories of the witchcraft, the positions, the training and slicing of my flesh. All to make me an assassin.

As I forced those memories away, I could understand why the Overlord destroyed the Temple and my friends. But I won't ever forgive him for killing my brother, my beautiful sweet, little brother. And that's why I'll help the Rebellion to kill the Overlord.

Someone touched my ass.

"Ello love," a creepy man said, grabbing me from behind.

Without even looking at the foul man, I knew it was the man who was staring at me earlier.

"Release me now and I let you live,"

"Come on Love, let's get down and dirty," he said, humping my back.

I spun around.

Whipping out my swords.

Slicing off his hands.

I grabbed his manhood.

I ripped it off.

He screamed as the blood rushed out of his lower body, turning the mud a beautiful deep rich red.

I did warn him.

Putting my swords away, I looked towards the entrance to the little town and saw the dancing had turned faster and more dramatic. I knew this town was a little strange and I didn't really want to be here.

Remembering the rumours of the witches and warlocks living in the town and their rituals to their gods, I knew I had to leave but I had to wait for the Hunters to arrive.

Someone screamed.

Knowing I was hardly in any danger for the next minute, I stared at the entrance of the town as the three shadowy male Hunters advanced into the town.

Ripping the souls out of the living.

I cocked my head at the new way to kill. I had no idea they could do that but now I really didn't want to be here.

One Hunter disappeared.

Someone slammed into me.

Tackling me to the ground.

I rolled up.

Holding up my arms.

I blocked a punch.

Then another.

Then another.

I kicked the person.

It was a Hunter.

I kicked him again.

His grip weakened.

I threw him off.

I punched him.

He jumped up.
Whipping out his hand.
Pain flooded me.
I felt my body being ripped apart.
I screamed.
I could feel him smile.
He gave twisted laugh.
I stopped screamed.
I focused.
I charged.
Knocking him to the ground.
I whistled.
Grabbing his head.
I smashed it to the ground.
My hands felt icy.
There was screaming.
The people were being slaughtered.
I heard something else.
There was singing.
There was shrieking.
The other Hunters were screaming.
The witches were attacking.
That's what the dancing was.
The Hunter whacked me off him.
I heard a horse.
The Hunter paused.
He screamed at me.
Whipping out his hand.
I jumped up.
Jumping into the air.

I landed on my horse.
I rushed away.
Leaving the Hunters to the witches.

CHAPTER 6

Commander Coleman took a long deep breath of the fresh, crisp air with hints of dry pine as he walked into the small ruined town.

Coleman hadn't been here before but he already knew that he wanted to be done with this place. The town was a small dusty ruined place with the rows of wooden houses infected with mould and damp and most of them were falling apart.

Even the semi-circle of houses that faced the entrance to the town was half destroyed. Coleman felt a wave of unease wash over him as he walked further.

Feeling the soft sandy ground crumble under his feet, Coleman focused on the surroundings and hoped this wasn't a trap of some sort.

It still bought Coleman comfort that he was wearing his large, thick grey armour that covered his entire body. Coleman didn't want to wear the helmet, it messed up his longish black hair.

As Coleman stopped in the centre of the circle of

houses, he noticed there were already a ring of guards stepping out of the half destroyed houses.

A part of Coleman wanted to laugh at the idea of calling them guards, they looked like young adults they were given a sword and sometimes a bow and told how to fire it. These weren't soldiers or guards.

If he was as callous as some of his friends, Coleman might have wanted to say these were hardly the people he wanted to help the Rebellion. But he hardly had a choice, if the Overlord was sending an army to kill them all. Then Coleman knew he couldn't be choosy about who he picked.

Hearing the guards click and mutter to themselves, Coleman tried to understand it but he couldn't. He remembered something about the clicking language of a northern tribe but he never learnt it. He didn't need to.

Yet as Coleman heard a few more clicks and the clicks getting faster and faster, he wished he had learnt.

Everything fell silent as Coleman smiled at a large heavy set man walking towards him. The Lord Baron Huin was a large man wearing thick leather armour that was far too small for him.

Coleman hoped the Lord Baron had better armour for when the Overlord came. The Baron couldn't last five minutes wearing that excuse of armour. But Coleman knew he was far too kind to say it.

Subtly looking around Coleman frowned slightly

as he couldn't see the Assassin anywhere. He really wanted her to be here and Coleman wanted to see (and feel) her long black leather trench coat and cloak. She always looked amazing in it.

Focusing on the Lord Baron's large, bearded face, Coleman smiled and nodded his respect towards the Lord.

"Commander Coleman. It's been a while," Huin said, his voice deep but sickly.

Coleman noticed the guards were still walking towards him.

"Lord Baron it is an honour to see you,"

"I would hope so. You own me,"

Coleman's eyes narrowed. "For what?"

"You costed me two thousand coins boy!"

Coleman shrugged. He had no clue what the Lord Baron was talking about. The guards were still getting closer.

"Last time we met. We raided a warehouse,"

Coleman frowned deepened. He knew where this was going. He remembered.

"Then you, Commander Coleman, burned all the fabrics and explosives and more!"

"That warehouse had to be destroyed,"

"Why! So you could save the innocent? I need to sell things and make money,"

"You would have sold it straight back to the Overlord,"

The Lord Baron smiled. "Given the right price of course. There are no sides in this war. Only money,"

Coleman spat on the ground. "That is where we are different. I want to protect the innocent. You want to kill them if it makes you money,"

The guards stopped a few metres from him.

"Coleman not all of us can live for free or live off pity donations,"

"Pity donations? People give us things because we are right. We want to make a difference,"

Huin and the guards busted out laughing.

"Coleman, people give you things because they pity the stupidity of your cause,"

A tiny part of Coleman wanted to nod at that. He knew the few free tribes that roamed the Kingdom thought his mission was silly and pointless. Even the Cities the Rebellion had claimed and freed didn't want the Rebellion there.

And that was something Coleman could never understand. He couldn't understand how people could allow themselves to be enslaved, tortured, forced to do horrific things and be okay with it.

"I will not stop trying to save them," Coleman said.

The Lord Baron nodded and waved away the Guards.

"One day you're values and your naivety will kill you,"

Coleman nodded. "That day maybe today or tomorrow, old friend,"

The Lord Baron walked up to Coleman. "You need by help, don't you?"

Coleman was about to speak but the Guards looked at something.

The Guards shouted.

They charged over to the entrance.

Coleman spun.

His eyes narrowed.

There was something coming for them.

The Guards aimed their arrows.

Then stopped.

Coleman cocked his head as he saw a strong brown horse ride into the small town without a rider.

He felt a blade against his throat and he smiled.

"You took your time, Assassin," Coleman said.

Feeling the blade leave his throat, Coleman turned around and his mouth almost dropped as he looked at the Assassin's long beautiful brown hair that looked so perfect and life filled.

Coleman felt his mouth drop slightly as he looked at her smooth, round, perfect face with her deep rich emerald eyes that he would happily get lost in. And he loved her black trench coat too.

Knowing that his beautiful Assassin was here, Coleman couldn't help but smile and imagine a time fighting side by side with her, and hopefully saving the Rebellion.

Then the question always would be, after that was done, would she want to stay around him? Or would she leave?

CHAPTER 7

As I took my cold blade away from Coleman's throat as he slowly turned around and smiled. Of course, he probably thought he was being careful and subtle in his love for me. But he really, really wasn't.

He must have loved the fact I had pulled down my black leather hood so my long brown hair covered my long black leather trench coat for to see. Some might say it was petty of me to make sure Coleman could see me. But a small part of me wanted to be admired, and it wanted to only be admired by Coleman.

Breathing in the fresh, crisp air with a hint of dry pine leaves, I have to admit he's great to look at too. But I'm naturally a lot better at containing my affection, the last thing I wanted was to give the Lord Baron a weakness to use against us. I wasn't having that!

But as I stared at Coleman's thick wonderful armour, I almost smiled at the memories of that amazing v-cut body beneath and those muscles. And I suppose his strong jawline and square face is another great feature of his.

As much as I didn't want to admit it, he was beautiful.

Making myself forget about him, I turn to face the overweight, ugly Lord Baron Huin, he hardly looked impressed to see me but I hardly cared. It would take me a second to chop off his head.

It would only take me an extra to spill his guts but I didn't want to ruin his horrific black leather armour. It was ugly, and against me, well, it would hardly offer him protection.

Feeling the soft sandy ground beneath me, I made a mental note about the ground in case I needed it. From past experience, I knew throwing sandy soil in people's eyes was effective. Forcing it down their throat, even more so.

As I subtly looked at the young guards dressed in rags that were eyeing me up and down, I put my little dagger away and I placed my hands on the warm hilts of my long swords. The young guards seemed to smile.

If I was a rude assassin, I probably would have called them out on their want for a challenge and called them stupid, for wanting to fight me. But I pretend to be polite most of the time.

Listening to the guards' click and mutter, I smiled at them as I heard them planning something. These pathetic guards probably didn't realise it was the

Temple of Assassins that created the clicking language and its various offshoots.

"It's nice to see you again," Coleman said.

It was times like this that I wished the Temple had let me keep most of humanity and my emotions. A normal person would have acted on the emotion in his voice, but I wanted to roll my eyes. I didn't have time for his affection.

I ignored him. "Baron, has Coleman told you the situation,"

"No, I was about to but that's when you arrived," Coleman said.

The guards clicked a little more. Something about an attack.

"I killed one of the Overlord's Puppet Kings. He told me the Overlord is sending an army to destroy the Rebellion. They're using the City of Death as a staging ground," I said.

The guards stopped clicking.

"And why do you both want me?"

"Because Huin, you have men and women. Fighters. We need them all," Coleman said.

I was a little impressed that he sounded forceful with that comment.

"What makes you think I will fight for the Rebellion? And you Assassin, what's your stake in this?" Huin asked.

I opened my mouth to speak but I closed it. I didn't know what I could say, I was an assassin who went around slaughtering targets for money. I couldn't say I was doing this out of the good of my black heart. I do have a reputation to protect.

So I said the only thing that sounded natural.

"Ask me again and I'll gut you," I said.

The Guards clicked a little faster. Something about prey. My hands tightened on my swords.

"Tell me, Assassin, Coleman, how many soldiers do you think the Overlord has?"

I shrugged. This wasn't my concern.

"We don't know but if they're using the City of Death then it's probably a few thousand," Coleman said.

"Exactly, Coleman. You actually think you can win. Flee. Go now. Leave your mountain and fight another day,"

I stepped forward. "What are you afraid of Huin? The once great Lord Baron, Ruler of the Huinian Kingdom and Family Ruler,"

As the Lord Baron's eyes narrowed and I saw rage build within him, I couldn't help but think about the Overlord and all the destruction he had done when he first took over the area fifty years ago. I was glad I wasn't alive to see that bloodshed.

I stared at Huin. "You had the choice to become a Puppet King for the Overlord. You could have ruled your region and lived. Why give it up?"

Huin's eyes widened, and I saw something in them. Conflict.

The guards started clicking more and more. Something about death and destruction and devastation.

"We have to go!" I shouted.

I grabbed Coleman.

We ran for my horse.

The three shadowy Hunters appeared.

All the guards and Hunters pointed their swords at us. I wasn't going to fight them all just yet.

Turning to face that traitorous Huin, I asked a simple question, my voice cold and flat and a bit psychotic.

"Why?"

"Because I never left the Overlord. I was given a higher purpose. Long live the Overlord!"

"Long Live the Overlord!" the guards shouted.

CHAPTER 8

Coleman stared at all the shiny swords pointing at him and his beautiful Assassin as they were surrounded by guards and now three shadowy Hunters.

His eyes widened as he looked at the Hunters, he couldn't believe how these things existed. Half human, half demon sounded made up but as he stared at their black shadowy faces and cloaks. Coleman knew they were real.

He knew they would kill him given the chance.

Taking a deep breath of the fresh air filled with the smell of dry pine leaves, Coleman felt the soft cold sandy ground under him. He needed to be prepared to move and run.

Coleman knew he couldn't afford to slip or fall during their escape. He had to be ready, his Assassin would be so he had to be ready. Coleman wasn't going to look like a fool in front of her.

As he turned to face that disgraceful Lord Baron

Huin, Coleman spat at him. Coleman always knew he had hated Huin, he was useless at the end of the day.

And it actually didn't surprise Coleman that Huin was working for the Overlord. It made sense why Huin got so annoyed at him for burning the explosives and other supplies.

Listening to the guards clicking and the cool wind gently howl past, Coleman placed his hand on his sword. But the Assassin's leathered gloved hands stopped him.

He knew the touch was through gloves, but it still made his stomach fill with butterflies.

He had to protect her.

"How much?" the Assassin asked.

Coleman wanted to kick himself at the Assassin asking that. He was the leader of the Rebellion and according to almost everyone he was the greater mind when it came to these things. So Coleman knew he should have asked that simple question first, he had to focus. He needed to act how he normally did, confident and firm.

"This wasn't about money Assassin. It's about the truth. The Truth you will die and the Rebellion will fail,"

The Assassin grinned at that. Coleman hoped she didn't think of him as a failure and a doomed cause.

"As I said Coleman, there are no sides. The Overlord is supreme and must be worshipped,"

Coleman laughed at that. "You really are deluded old friend,"

The Assassin looked around.

"No Coleman, it is you who are fooled. You cannot win. The Overlord will lead the charge and you will dead by his righteous hand,"

My eyes narrowed. "What? The Overlord has left the Capital for the first time in thirty years,"

Huin nodded.

Coleman looked away from the Lord Baron, he couldn't understand this. The Overlord was meant to be this god amongst men, a slaughterer, a butcherer, a master of arms. Coleman couldn't let his Rebels face him, they would die. Something Coleman couldn't allow. He had to do something.

The Assassin looked around.

"Baron Huin. Where is he?" she asked.

"The City of Death,"

Coleman was about to speak but he noticed the air behind him felt colder than before. He turned around and frowned when he saw the Hunters were getting closer to them.

Placing his hand firmly on his sword, Coleman said.

"Tell them to back off,"

Huin laughed. "I don't control them. I wouldn't dare offend the Will of the Overlord,"

The Lord Baron knelt on the floor and bowed to the Hunters. Seeing the Assassin was licking her lips at the kneeling Huin, Coleman hated to think what she was planning.

"Assassin dearest, are you done scheming?"

"In a moment," the Assassin said.

Coleman looked at the traitorous Baron and he was a little surprised Huin didn't seem concerned by that simple question. Was he really that silly?

The Assassin's eyes narrowed. "Huin, how did the Hunters know we were coming? You would have turned us in any way. But even you wouldn't have the Hunters come here,"

Coleman rolled his eyes as he saw Huin given a slight nod, to Coleman that added to the weirdness of it. Why would Huin fight for the Overlord if he was so scared of him?

"The Hunters grabbed the bird you sent. They read the note, not changing it and sent the Rebellion another bird,"

The Assassin smiled and nodded.

Coleman looked at her. "Done now?"

"Of course," she said smiling. "Ready?"

The Hunters tensed.

Coleman nodded.

The Assassin rammed her sword into Huin.

His corpse fell forward.

Coleman whipped out his sword.

Charging at the Hunters.

He jumped on one.

Icy pain shot into him.

He slammed his fists into one.

The Assassin slaughtered the guards.

They screamed.

Their bodies shattered.

Their blood gushed out.
Coleman jumped up.
Swinging his sword.
The Hunter met it.
Lightning shot out.
Coleman's sword glowed.
He jumped back.
The Hunters charged.
The Assassin grabbed him.
They ran to the horse.
The air buzzed.
It crackled.
Lightning shot towards them.
The ground exploded.
Kicking up sand.
Coleman covered his eyes.
He tripped.
Falling to the ground.
He opened his eyes.
The Assassin kept running.
The Hunters touched him.
Coleman screamed in agony.
Crippling pain filled him.
He felt his soul being drained.
Coleman swung his sword.
Slicing a Hunter.
The Hunter shrieked.
The air crackled.
Coleman swung it as hard as he could.
It sliced into the shadow.

The Hunter fell.
The other two released him.
Coleman rushed forward.
The Assassin rode to him.
Grabbing him.
Throwing him over the horse.
The Hunters screamed.
The air crackled.
They were gone.

CHAPTER 9

I love watching.

Some people would say that I watch too much or for too long before moving on them. I disagree as I know these people clearly aren't assassins or they're only wanna be assassins, I remember at the Temple of Assassins that the longest a Master Assassin had waited and watched before killing a target was five years. I don't think I would watch for that long, but watching is critical.

Staring out over the massive grey sandstone valley between our mountain and the City of Death, my eyes narrowed and I blocked out all the sounds around me, from the singing of birds as the sun set to the rustling that Coleman was making.

A part of me wanted to talk to him but I oddly enough felt nervous about it. Just the thought of having a real conversation with that beautiful, handsome man made a drop of sweat roll down my back.

I know it's stupid and I know I shouldn't be like this but it's happening. This is why I like to work alone and I hate working with other people, because sometimes these other people are beautiful, handsome and stunning.

And I don't need them distracting me from my work.

Focusing on the City of Death ahead, I understood why it was perfect for mining. The massive black rocky hill in the middle of the valley shone slightly in the dying sunlight, it was rich in ore that was a fact.

I moaned under my breath as I couldn't see anything more than that. I hated how the City of Death was a City inside a black rocky hill. The only thing I could see of the City was the top of a spire. Maybe a Church, maybe a watchtower. I couldn't tell.

Breathing in the cold, crisp evening air, I pulled my long black leather trench coat and cloak over me tight. The last thing I wanted was to be remembered as the best assassin who didn't die from a blade or a bow, but died by freezing on a mountain.

I felt Coleman walk up to me before he stopped about a metre from me. I didn't need to turn around to see he was probably considering whether or not he should comfort me or hug me for warmth.

A part of me wondered if I wanted it, Coleman was handsome and he did have large strong muscles that were probably very warm. But could I allow him to see me vulnerable? What if he tried to kill me?

I almost laughed at myself but I remembered a game or mission we played through our years at the

Temple. We were to get with people we found attractive then try to kill them when the time was right, and if we died or we killed them we won the game, and the dead one wasn't a worthy assassin.

That was fun! Twisted but fun!

As I knew I was being silly and acting strange, I was about to turn around but Coleman sat next to me. He looked so handsome in his thick, heavy metal armour but I stared into the deep emerald eyes and I relaxed. I felt... safe. The first time in a long time.

"Thanks for saving me again," Coleman said.

I smiled. "You didn't do so bad. You saved yourself sort of,"

As bad as that must have sounded (I knew it sounded cold) Coleman didn't seem upset or put off.

"I felt something was off so I was glad to get your note,"

"Coleman, please I know you want to say something,"

He took a deep breath.

"I've missed you,"

A small part of me wanted to say the same but I couldn't get the idea of him wanting more from me out of my head. I liked Coleman a lot and he was handsome but I couldn't deal with those feelings right now. I had to complete my mission and save the innocent rebels that (damn them) I care about.

"I missed you too but I am an Assassin,"

"So?"

"Coleman, I kill people. You lead them. nothing

can ever happen between us,"

I rolled my eyes as I realised that went from letting him down gently to throwing him away quickly.

Coleman smiled. "So you do have feelings for me?"

For some reason I smiled at his question, he wasn't giving up on this strange fantasy of his and I respected that.

Coleman leant in closer to me. I wasn't going to move away, a part of me wanted Coleman just for a moment, just so I could always have this memory of a kiss before I forced myself to go back to my assassin ways.

But that wasn't fair on him, he wanted a moment to happen and last forever. I couldn't hurt Coleman like that, he was too good of a man for that.

I pulled away.

"Coleman, I'm not going to ask that,"

He nodded, a little sadness in his eyes, but he seemed okay.

Looking out over the valley, I pointed towards the City of Death with little fires lighting it up now as night descended.

"We need to check it out," Coleman said.

I was a little surprised by his bravery at that suicidal mission, but I respected him.

"If the Overlord's there. He'll be guarded," I said.

"I'm not worried about the Overlord. We need

to know what we're dealing with,"

"Wait, you don't want to kill the Overlord. This is the first shot the Rebellion's had in thirty years,"

Coleman nodded and shrugged.

"Fine, Coleman. We'll do a quick sweep and escape back to the rebel base," I said.

Watching those deep emerald eyes nod and agree with me, we stood up and started to ride down the mountain.

I just didn't have the heart to tell him I was an assassin and I never miss an opportunity to kill someone. Even the Overlord.

CHAPTER 10

Commander Coleman crouched as him and the Assassin advanced in the City of Death. When they stopped behind a large boulder Coleman looked around, he wanted to study every detail.

He wasn't impressed that the two of them were deep within the City of Death without any help. Coleman hated the look of the sharp, rough black rocks all around them.

The odd thing about the City of Death was, it was the only City in the Kingdom to be built inside a mountain that Coleman wondered whether it was a dormant volcano. Since most of the City was inside a large dip in the mountain.

That fact still didn't make Coleman feel any better as he focused on the sharp, rough black rocks that formed the slopes. He hated the idea of slipping and the sharp rocks ripping into his flesh.

Breathing in the freezing cold air with hints of coal and smoke, Coleman popped his head out from the boulder and studied their surroundings. He cocked his head as he realised there was no one here.

The sounds of a fire roaring in the distance, probably one of the distant tunnels, was the only sound here. Considering there was meant to be thousands of angry Overlord men here, it was too quiet and empty.

Coleman's eyes narrowed as he looked on the large patch of smooth flat black stone that made some kind of floor at the bottom of the dip, with nothing else there except a wooden hut in the middle.

A small part of Coleman wanted to go inside but something felt very off. It made no sense for the army not to be here with all the intelligence and information saying so. It made even less sense to Coleman why the Overlord would tell all his men one thing, but keep the actual army in another location.

The army had to be here. But they weren't.

Coleman placed a hand on the icy cold hilt of his sword and took a freezing cold breath again. He was going to be prepared.

Turning his head slightly, Coleman looked at his beautiful Assassin crouching there in her beautifully long black leather trench coat and black hood. Coleman loved it how she was almost invisible in the darkness.

For a moment he remembered what she had said to him about a relationship. Coleman smiled at her confessing (in a weird way) she had feelings for him and that had filled him with happiness. He had been wanting to hear that for so long.

Now he just needed to convince her it was okay if they got together and it wasn't some weakness to be used against her. And Coleman also wondered what her name was, it had to be a beautiful name knowing her and she had never told anyone.

Hearing the Assassin move into the open, Coleman carefully followed and he whipped out his sword. He followed her to the wooden hut as she inspected it.

Coleman wanted to kick him, he knew she wouldn't come here for a quick scouting mission like he ordered. If it was anyone else, he would have been firmer and he would have left now. But Coleman knew he cared about the Assassin too much and now he feared it might come back to bite him.

Seeing the bright orange light of fire at the end of a nearby tunnel, Coleman felt his stomach tighten. This was too close for comfort, one sound and Coleman knew the enemy would hear.

"What are you doing?" Coleman asked, his voice barely audible.

"I'm doing my job,"

"No your job is to-"

"Coleman I am an assassin. I kill people,"

"If the Overlord is in there let's be prepared,"

The Assassin shook her head.

"Assassin this is not an argument. We are leaving," Coleman said, firmly.

The Assassin stopped and slowly turned to him.

As Coleman stared into her cold, dark eyes he felt a drop of sweat run down his forehead.

"You're. Ordering. Me?"

Coleman had to stand up to her. He was not a coward.

"Yes. We are leaving. We have what we-"

The Assassin slapped him.

"I am not yours Coleman. I am not one of your Rebels. I am not your girlfriend. I am not property. I thought you were different,"

Coleman felt his spirit and body lower a little as he listened to those words, at first he thought the Assassin was taunting or mocking his feelings for her, but as he listened to her words they weren't mocking or judgemental. They were truly sad with an edge of disappointment.

As he watched the Assassin scout out the rest of the wooden hut, Coleman wanted to kick himself hard. He wasn't the bossy, overprotective type, he always worked with his friends.

Coleman walked over to the Assassin. "I'm sorry,"

The Assassin was silent.

"I didn't mean to be overprotective,"

The Assassin hissed.

"I-"

Rocks fell down the slopes.

Coleman looked up. Shadows were moving.

He raised his sword.

The Assassin jumped up.

Swords raised.

The sound of tens upon tens of heavily armed men and women marching out of the tunnels made Coleman roll his eyes as him and the Assassin lowered their weapons.

They both knew it was useless fighting this many warriors but as the warriors surrounded them and took their weapons.

Coleman's stomach twisted and sweat dropped off him as he saw a tall man in thin glowing silver armour.

The Overlord had come.

CITY OD DEATH

CHAPTER 11

My mouth dropped as I stared at the tall angelic man who walked towards us. I could only stare as I looked at his smooth youthful skin and his killer smile that would make women fall over him and straight men gay. His long blond hair was stunning and I felt all energy from my body leave me.

Of course, as soon as I realised this, I stopped thinking like a common woman and instead my assassin training kicked in. I wasn't sure what magic this idiot was using, but it was powerful I'll give him that.

I wasn't a fan was of thin silver glowing armour. I would probably guess it was a combination of normal steel armour and some kind of magical blend. I doubted my swords would pierce it, so I'm afraid I might have to leave him.

I so badly wanted to smash his skull in.

Turning my attention to the guards and warriors, I smiled at each of them as I looked at their thick grey armour and their longswords, bows and even something called a crossbow.

This killing was going to be fun.

My smile deepened as I noticed the sharp black rocks on the slopes of the City of Death, I wouldn't object to ripping someone's flesh on them.

The sounds of clicking and metal moving made me shook my head, I couldn't believe no one knew that the clicking language was made by the Temple of Assassins. Ridiculous!

Staring at the warriors, I clocked their eyes were wide and focused. They were scared of me and I loved that. So to show how contempt I was, I took a long freezing cold breath (almost coughed at the hints of smoke) and breathed it out. Forming a long column of vapour, as simple as it sounds I smiled as the warriors took a tiny step back.

The Overlord clapped his hands.

The warriors pointed their swords at us.

They advanced.

As we walked backwards I heard some fool open the door to the wooden hut, I hadn't noticed the door was iron before. We walked into the hut and the door slammed shut with a heavy click of the lock.

I ignored the wooden hut for the most part. It was a small empty wooden room with rough wooden walls.

Instead I focused on the iron door and I stared at the three bars running across the top forming a window of sorts.

The Overlord stepped in front and smiled. That stupid killer smile, I was definitely going to slice that smile open at some point.

"At Jasmine you are safe," the Overlord said.

My heart dropped and my mouth fell to the floor as he said my name. The name only I truly knew, well, there was a reason he knew but I hated him.

If I could, my hands would shoot through these bars and rip his throat out right now.

"Jasmine?" Coleman asked.

I wasn't even going to look at that beautiful idiot who felt so overprotective of me like I was his property.

"Oh yes Commander Coleman, Jasmine is her name. Didn't she tell you? She probably didn't even tell you I'm her father,"

My eyes widened as he dared to speak those words. I was going to shred his skin one day.

"You are not my father. You threw me in a river. My family is not you,"

The Overlord smiled at that. It took everything I had not to lash out.

"I am still your father. I raised you for a month before I threw you in that river. It's a shame you didn't drown but here we are,"

I could feel Coleman coming closer to me. If he hugged me, I swear to the gods I'll punch him. (I didn't want to though, I didn't want to slap him either)

"Jasmine, your adoptive parents and brothers and

sisters are dead. The parents burned screaming out your name as they tried to warn you I was coming,"

My eyes narrowed.

"And well, you know what happened to your true brother and your adoptive sisters,"

I walked straight up to the metal bars. "Why kill us? Why threw us in the river?"

The Overlord pressed his head against the bars. Our noses touched.

"Because… it was fun,"

I chomped his nose off.

Spitting it on the ground.

The Overlord shot back.

Laughing.

The bastard was laughing!

I looked at Coleman for a brief moment, a small part of me wanted to just fall into his strong muscular arms and kiss him.

But as I looked at him, he wasn't staring at me. those beautiful bright emerald eyes were narrowed and rageful as he stared at the Overlord.

Maybe he wasn't completely head over heels in love with me (thankfully) and maybe he could function around me. That would be nice.

"Commander Coleman, Jasmine, I presume you are both wondering why the City is so empty,"

"You threw them in the river?" I asked.

The Overlord wiped another stream of blood from his nose and smiled.

"Three thousand men. That is the number that is

heading for your Rebels,"

I wanted to smash his head in even more now. The Rebels couldn't defend against that number. Then a silly wave of emotion washed over me as I remembered why I was trapped here in this wooden hut, because I cared about them and their cause. I knew I was going to help them no matter what, I just had to get out of here first.

As the Overlord started to walk away, the Overlord said a final thing, I hated how cold and flat his voice was.

"And thank the traitor for me. I look forward to using your tunnels,"

I turned to Coleman and my eyebrows rose as I saw his face turn deadly white and cold, fearful sweat dropped down his face. (Not very sexy but this wasn't a sexy moment)

"What is it?" I asked.

"The tunnels lead them into the heart of the base. If they get to the tunnels, we'll lose before the battle begins,"

Listening to beautiful Coleman said that didn't make me nervous or scared, it made me excited. I always loved a challenge, and unlike Coleman, my bastard father and their little toy soldiers, I loved impossible odds and at the end of the day, war was a game.

So let the games begin and let the sword fall.

CHAPTER 12

Commander Coleman stared at the chunk of the Overlord's nose that laid on the cold, rocky ground as he tried not to panic. He couldn't believe there was a traitor in the Rebellion, he loved every one of those Rebels like they were his family. The idea of one of them being a traitor was disgraceful.

Looking over to his beautiful Assassin, Coleman knew for a fact that if she didn't get to the traitor before him, he would end the traitor. Hopefully, in a way that make Jasmine proud but as long as the traitor died Coleman didn't care.

As he stared at the Assassin's beautiful black leather trench coat and black cloak, Coleman couldn't understand her past. He never in a million years would have thought she was the Overlord's biological daughter, and that her name was Jasmine. It was a beautiful name perfect for the beautiful woman it belonged to, but Coleman wasn't sure it was the most Assassin-y name.

Taking a breath of the freezing cold air that reminded him of eating roasted hog in the snowy mountains a few years ago, Coleman looked around for a way to escape, they had to get out of here and warn the Rebellion and warn them about the tunnels.

Coleman frowned as all he saw were cold, unloved wooden walls and that ugly heavy iron door. They were unarmed and Coleman felt like an utter failure, he was a failure.

For his entire life since his father had passed on the cause to him (He didn't even know his father was alive until he rescued Coleman from the City of Pleasure), Coleman had fought the Overlord, killed his men and fought every ally the Overlord had. But as he stood in that cold wooden hut, a small part of him knew it was all for nothing. Coleman took a deep cold breath as he realised he was never going to escape and all his friends would die, even worse the Kingdom would never be free of the Overlord's taint. They would all be doomed.

Then Coleman's frowned deepened when he stared at the utterly stunning and beautiful Jasmine, who was looking at something near the door, if there were any gods or goddesses all Coleman would ask is if they would take him instead of her.

Coleman didn't want Jasmine to die.

The sounds of the wind howling across the City of Death made Coleman shiver a little. He stood up to go to the Assassin and-

A massive roar ripped through the City.

Three men screamed.

Coleman stopped and looked at the Assassin. As he saw she wasn't bothered, Coleman shrugged and went over to her.

"Are you done with your pity party?" Jasmine asked.

"Yes. But it wasn't a pity party I was planning our escape,"

She laughed. "Sure you were. Help me with the door,"

Coleman cocked his head as he saw the Assassin had cracked the wooden frame slightly. He smiled at her brilliance, he never would have thought of that. Why try and break through steel when you can break the frame instead?

The Assassin took a few steps back. Coleman joined her. She nodded.

They charged into the door.

It cracked.

They charged again.

It cracked louder.

They looked at each other.

They flew at the door.

The wood snapped.

The weight of the door did the rest.

The door smashed to the ground.

Coleman stormed out.

Checking the surroundings, but they stopped and Coleman's mouth dropped slightly when he saw two shredded bodies of guards. Their skulls were shattered. Their flesh flayed.

Coleman went over to them and picked up their swords and two for the Assassin. She nodded her thanks.

A roar ripped through the City.

More people screamed.

The Assassin ran up the slopes.

Coleman followed her.

A claw grabbed him.

He swung his sword.

Something shrieked.

Coleman looked.

A massive scaly bear stared at him.

The bear attacked.

It roared.

Coleman ran.

The bear whacked him to the ground.

Coleman swung.

Slashing the Bear.

Green blood splashed everywhere.

Covering Coleman's legs.

The Bear flew at him.

Slicing into him.

Rich red blood poured out.

The Bear rose up.

Exposing its underbelly.

Coleman slashed.

He rammed his sword into it.

Nothing happened.

The underbelly was armoured.

Coleman swore.

The bear stomped.

Coleman rolled.

The Bear slashed his back.

Destroying Coleman's armour.

Coleman spun.

Jumping up.

The Bear swung.

Coleman swung.

Slicing off the Bear's hand.

The Bear shrieked.

Green blood gushed out.

It fell to the ground.

Coleman thrusted his sword into the Bear's skull.

Twisting it.

Allowing the icy cold air to wrap around his body, he heard someone clapping at him and he looked at the smiling Assassin. Coleman gave her a bow and she smiled.

As he started to walk up the sharp, deadly slopes of the City of Death, at least he now knew why the City was called what it was, but most importantly he had made his beautiful Assassin smile. That was too precious for words.

Maybe there was a possible future, but first Coleman had to warn the Rebellion and defeat an army.

CHAPTER 13

After I whistled for my horse and we rode back to the rebels, and personally I was amazed at how slow the Overlord's army was but as I watched and remembered how strict they were on keeping their so-called perfect formations. I understood why they were so slow, if one person was slow then everyone else had to be slow to keep their *perfect* formation.

As I sat on a cold black leather chair I allowed it to mould to my body and relax a little, as I focused on the other people that were sat around the large wooden table in front of us.

I forget what Coleman had called this room we were in but I didn't like it. I hated the coldness and soullessness of it with its smooth yellow rock walls and white ceiling. It wasn't exactly what I expected from a group of Rebels that had lived here for over forty years.

Breathing in the smells of fake perfumes and sweat and body odour and listening to the sounds of the people talk, mutter and moan at each other, I knew straight away these other people sitting with me were true rebels, or at least Rebels that were high ranking.

I made sure I pulled my black leather trench coat tight and made sure my face was well and truly covered by my black hood, then I started to do what I did best.

Study people.

Looking at each of their faces, I guessed all I would have to do to kill each one would be a quick slice of my blades across their throats. It wouldn't take much and I was glad Coleman wasn't a mind reader, but these thoughts were necessary considering there's a traitor here.

My eyes narrowed on each of them and I made sure I studied their faces. I presume the first two mortals I looked at were sisters with their blond perfectly straight hair, I never liked people who tried too hard to look good.

When I turned to the other man at the table my eyes narrowed as much as they could as I noticed the man with his black beard and scars was staring at me. How dare someone stare at me, who does he think he is?

The sounds of their talking and annoying voices stopped as beautiful Commander Coleman with his amazing bright emerald eyes started catching them up on the situation.

I have to give him credit where it's due, it actually made the story sound gripping filled with slaughter and adventure. Of course the slaughter was all done by me, and with each detail of me ramming my sword into someone, the more concerned looks I got.

Normally I would growl or do something to make these fools scared of me but at that moment all I cared about was looking at Coleman. Admiring his smooth amazing face and trying to catch glimpses of those amazing emerald eyes.

"Coleman this assassin shouldn't be in here. She's a murderer, a threat to us, we need to stop her and-"

I raised a warning gloved finger to her. "I promised myself I wouldn't kill any Rebels. So don't tempt me,"

"Listen to her Barbic," Coleman said.

Barbic. Interesting name, I needed to remember that for later.

"Come on bossie what tha plan?"

"Abbic, it's simple. Gather the forces outside the mountain and we'll fight there. I don't want them anywhere near the base," Coleman said.

I nodded, I supposed it was a good plan but I needed to think of something. As much as I love these Rebels and Coleman (of course), my faith in their fighting abilities was limited to say the least, I just had to find a weakness in the enemy.

"That a good plan boss,"

"Thank you, Dragnist. Did you block the tunnels like I asked?"

Dragnist nodded but I hated how he kept staring at me, then as he licked his lips I knew exactly why he was staring at me. I don't know what it is with men with assassins. Half of them are turned off, half of them are very turned on.

They're a nightmare I swear.

"Bossie what ya gonna do about that campy," Abbic asked.

I leant forward. "What camp?"

Barbic rolled her eyes. "I told you she was useless,"

"Say that again and I'll prove how useless I am throwing a knife,"

Barbic rolled her eyes again. Part of me wondered if she was from a posh upper class family who thought everyone who wasn't upper class was trash, I certainly killed enough of those people before. It wouldn't surprise me if she thought like that.

"What camp?" I asked again.

"Well Missy whenever one of these armies pop along those bossies set up a massive campy like our base-y,"

My eyes narrowed on this Abbic character and I allowed my mouth to give a small smile.

"And if the Overlord was leading the attack he would be there right?"

"Course Missy. I bet ya money on it,"

My smile deepened as I imagined taking all her money because I knew for a fact the Overlord was long gone. I'm not sure how I know but leading an army to crush a little Rebel base, that didn't sound like a reason to leave the Capital for the first time in thirty years.

I truly think he left the Capital to trap me and see if this mysterious Assassin was his daughter. I... think that's why he did it.

Now I know the Overlord is my father (I always knew but it feels weird to have it confirmed), I don't know whether or not to hate myself. But whatever happens I will be the child that kills the father.

"Assassin something you want to share? Coleman asked with a massive beautiful smile.

"Will you all be able to draw up the battle plans with me?"

Coleman looked at the others. "Yes, but why?"

I looked at the ground then I managed to force myself to look at him.

"I have to go,"

"Typical, utterly useless. This almighty-"

I threw a knife at her.

The knife slammed just behind her ear.

Barbic went silent.

Turning my attention back to the beautiful Coleman, I had no idea it was going to be this difficult to say I wanted to leave and not see him for a day or two.

That's if I survived.

As much as I've hated his affection and how much he cares about me (I mean come on he's a bit possessive at times), I actually feel like I'm going to miss him.

Staring into those bright emerald eyes, I stepped

closer to him.

"I have to go to this camp. If there's someone in charge there. I have to assassinate him, it's the only way to keep you, the Rebels safe,"

I loved seeing Coleman smile at my words, his eyes softened and he looked like he wanted to kiss me. A small part of me wanted that too but I wouldn't kiss him in front of his… whatever these fools called themselves.

"Stay safe, Coleman. I need you when I return," I asked, not sure what I meant by that.

He smiled at me. "Stay safe yourself,"

Turning away and fighting away the urge to kiss him goodbye, I stormed out of the meeting and left those fools to plan their deaths.

Now I had to do my bit to make sure not all of them died.

CHAPTER 14

Commander Coleman's mouth dropped open as he felt the soft valley ground move under his feet and he looked straight ahead into the deadly jaws of the enemy.

He stared at three thousand angry, rageful soldiers march towards him, Coleman hated their cold black armour. The enemy wasn't moving slowly or quickly, they moved at a pace that allowed the Rebels' minds to lead them into a spiral of despair.

Coleman forced thoughts of his own death, the slaughter of his friends and the death of his Jasmine out of his mind.

He couldn't have those thoughts inside him, Coleman had to lead his people, even if it was to a mindless, pointless massacre.

Wearing his thick, perfectly shiny metal armour with his long sword and dagger, Coleman hoped he was ready for the fight of his lifetime. This wasn't a fight about freedom, their cause and defending the innocent.

It was a fight to stop their annihilation.

Breathing in a cold, icy breath of the piney valley air, Coleman took out his sword and pointed it into the sky. He didn't know why he did it, he just hoped it would inspire his Rebels.

The sounds of the enemy screaming and shouting filled the valley, Coleman could see his Rebels shake and shiver as they looked at the foe.

Coleman had no idea if they would win today but he had to try.

Looking at the surrounding sharp razor mountains lining the edges of the valley, Coleman hoped the enemy wasn't trying to outflank them, he had sent Rebels to guard the mountain passes but Coleman had a feeling their corpses were already being devoured by wolves and flies.

Staring dead ahead at the approaching army, Coleman felt his stomach twist as he worried about his friends but most of all Jasmine, he wouldn't have anything done against her.

But as Coleman stared with anger and rage at the enemy, he knew the only thing he could do to protect her, was to fight and try and buy her as much time as possible.

Coleman took a deep piney breath and he thrusted his sword into the air.

He charged.

A thousand rebels charged.

Rebel archers fired.

A storm of arrows rained down.
Stabbing into the foes.
Slashing at their flesh.
Lashing their armour.
Few corpses dropped.
Coleman kept charging.
A trumpet sounded.
The enemy charged.
Three thousand foes flew at them.
Coleman's heart thumped inside him.
He whipped out his dagger.
The two armies clashed.
They slaughtered each other.
Swords swung.
Cracking armour.
Cracking skulls.
Shattering bones.
Slicing into flesh.
Blood gushed out.
Limbs were severed.
Heads were chopped off.
Coleman charged forward.
Ramming his sword into a man.
Two foes swung at Coleman.
He ducked.
Jumping up.
Decapitating the two foes.
Coleman ducked again.
Three swords flew past.
Arrows flew down.

Stabbing the foes.
They fell.
Coleman jumped on their heads.
The enemy advanced.
Jumping into the air.
Firing crossbows.
Slaughtering Rebels.
Rebel chests exploded.
Coleman rolled his eyes.
The enemy landed.
Coleman rolled forward.
Thrusting the dagger into one chest.
He leapt up.
Swinging his sword in one bloody arc.
Slashed throats flooded out blood.
The corpses dropped.
Coleman looked around.
Hundreds of rebels were dead.
Their corpses smashed into the soil.
Rebels screamed.
Their blood turned the ground red.
Coleman ducked.
Slashing the chest of an enemy.
Enemy archers fired.
Coleman ran.
Arrows slammed around him.
He heard the arrows scream towards him.
Rebels screamed in agony.
Pain crippled them.
Coleman knew he had to go.

This battle was lost.
He had to retreat.
An arrow touched his ear.
Coleman spun.
An archer chased him.
Coleman stopped.
Throwing a dagger.
The archer's head split.
Coleman ran.
He ordered his forces back.
This was a stupid idea.
He had to fight the enemy inside the base.
More rebels screamed.
Their bodies ripped open.
Their guts pouring out.

Over five hundred Rebels laid dead at Coleman's feet.

CHAPTER 15

My feet silently moved over the hard rough black mountain as I advanced toward my target. I knew the enemy weren't going to set up camp nearby so I had to ride for another hour then I travelled the rest of the way on foot.

Stopping, I pulled my long black leather trench coat and black hood over myself as I smiled. I loved the pathetic look of their little military camp with their bright white and red canvas tents.

As I stared at it from the mountain top, the hot sun beamed down on me but the cold icy wind destroyed that heat quickly. I loved the cold.

My smile deepened as my eyes narrowed on my target, I couldn't believe how pathetic the enemy had been. It's one thing to send three thousand soldiers to destroy some (equally pathetic) Rebels but it's another thing to leave your main camp unprotected.

My eyes scanned the large white and red canvas tents with them neatly organised in neat rows upon rows. It was easily large enough for four thousand soldiers.

I wouldn't be surprised if the Overlord sent a thousand warriors to secure the mountain passages.

Listening to the screaming and shouting in the distance I knew the battle had begun but as silly as it sounded drops of sweat rolled down my spine.

Before this City of Death business, I would have called it a weakness or me being silly. But now I know it's because I care, not just about the so-called cause and my beautiful Coleman with his amazing emerald eyes, but because I feel like I have a... family there.

Discounting that Barbic woman, they like me and respect me, that's all I want. Maybe I could stay there when this is all over. Maybe.

Looking at the massive white and red tent in the middle of the camp, I silently leant forward as I tried to study it. It was some kind of major tent of course but I couldn't tell if the Overlord or anyone important was inside.

Then I remembered one simple fact. There were enough supplies here for four thousand soldiers, even if there wasn't a major pawn of the Overlord inside, that didn't matter.

If the camp was destroyed, let's say, by a horrific fire the enemy would be easy pickings. Especially without any sort of protection at night time.

I couldn't help but smile at the idea of slashing their throat as they slept. Oh yes, something was going to be done about these tents.

The sound of crackling fire made me turn my attention back to the military camp. My eyes narrowed as I saw those foul black armoured guards stand around little fire pits like they were perfectly safe and there were in no danger whatsoever.

A massive grin broke out on my face as I swore I was going to prove them very wrong indeed.

If they were going to slaughter the Rebels and turn the ground red with their blood. Then I suppose it's only fair if I do the same, right?

CHAPTER 16

Commander Coleman took a cold deep breath of the piney mountain air as he crouched waiting for the enemy to come.

He really hoped this wasn't going to be another silly choice on his part but he knew it had been right to fight the enemy in the open valley, this was the Rebel home base, Coleman wasn't going to let some ugly Overlord soldiers in there.

But now he had no choice.

His eyes narrowed on the cold hard black rocks below him as Coleman grabbed a rough rock in his hand. Looking at his friends around him, all in their leather and metal armour, Coleman prepared to smash the enemy with the rocks.

A small part of him knew this was useless but even if he only killed ten of the enemy then that was good. It meant ten less foes to kill his rebels. He didn't want any of them to die.

Coleman raised his head and nodded to the

rebels on the other side of the mini canyon that the enemy would have to walk through to get into the base. The other rebels smiled back, they were excited, Coleman was excited.

Remembering the other rebels boiling up some oil and other surprises to welcome the enemy, Coleman smile only deepened, victory was a certainty.

The strong smell of dry pine started to turn into the disgusting smell of sweat, blood and flesh. Coleman took a deep breath. The enemy were coming.

Listening to the sounds of excitement and hope of his friends all around him made Coleman hopeful of the battle ahead and-

Thick black armoured warriors stormed into the mini-canyon. Their swords and crossbows raised, ready to kill.

Coleman threw the stone.

It smashed into a head.

Crushing it.

Blood spattered up the rock.

The rebels attacked.

Launching rock after rock.

The enemy was slaughtered.

Their armour dented.

Their skulls smashed.

Their spirits melted.

Coleman smiled.

He picked up another rock.

He threw it.

The rock stopped.
It floated there.
It flew at Coleman.
He ducked.
His eyes widened.
Screams filled the air.
Coleman spun around.
Three black cloaked witches stormed at him.
Coleman whipped out his sword.
The witches laughed.
They shrieked.
Rebels charged at them.
Swinging their sword.
The witches twisted their hands.
Snapping the Rebels necks.
Coleman froze.
The witches gripped Coleman.
Coleman struggled.
He tried to scream.
He tried to warn the others.
All were useless.
The other rebels went to help.
The witches' eyes narrowed.
The rebels took out their swords.
Ramming them into their own chests.
The corpses smiled as they fell.
Coleman's blood boiled.
Rageful filled him.
How dare they!
Coleman roared.

Breaking free.
The witches' eyes widened.
Coleman charged.
The witches attacked.
Fireballs flew at Coleman.
Lightning shot at him.
Coleman kept charging.
He swung his sword.
Thrusting it into a witch.
The witch's corpse turned to smoke.
The other witches screamed in terror.
More rebels ran at the witches.
Coleman smiled.
Pots of boiling oil were coming.
The rebels threw the oil.
The witches thrusted out their hands.
Boiling oil stopped in the air.
Coleman ran over.
He knew what was going to happen.
The witches smiled.
Boiling hot oil splashed over the rebels.
Burning them.
They screamed in utter agony.
The witches waved their hands.
Throwing the rebels miles.
Shattering their bodies.
Coleman hated this.
He hated losing.
Coleman flew at the witches.
Torrents of fire licked his flesh.

Coleman kept charging.
The witches shot lightning at him.
He ducked.
The enemy were advancing.
Coleman heard their screams.
Coleman swung his sword.
A witch ducked.
The other didn't.
Slicing into her head.
The witch shrieked.
Coleman kicked her.
She fell to the ground.
Coleman slammed his sword into her throat.
Black blood gushed out.
An arm grabbed him.
Getting him into a headlock.
His neck burned.
The witch whispered ancient words.
Coleman hissed.
He whipped up his sword.
Slicing his own ear.
The witch gasped.
Her grip loosened.
Coleman whacked her.
Throwing her to the ground.
He charged over.
Stomping on her head.
Coleman ran towards the base.
It was filled with the enemy.
Rebel corpses laid everywhere.

The enemy hacked his friends apart.

Limbs littered the ground.

Coleman saw a mass of rebels tens of metres away.

They were protecting the door to the inner base.

He waved at them.

A sword swung at him.

Coleman ducked.

Slashing the throat of the enemy.

Coleman spun back.

The rebels had seen him.

They were retreating.

Rebels were pouring into the door of the base.

Coleman charged towards the rebels.

Every rebel was inside.

The door started to shut.

They wouldn't shut the door on him.

Coleman jumped over corpses.

He leapt over the enemy.

Swords swung at him.

Coleman dodged.

He kept running.

He didn't want to be trapped out here.

He had to go.

He had to survive.

He had to get inside.

CHAPTER 17

Making sure my entire body was covered in my long black leather trench coat and definitely making sure my black hood covered my face, I stepped into the main camp.

I made sure I looked confident and like I was meant to be here (that's the key with most infiltrations) as I slowly walked through the main camp.

Now I was here I didn't mine the large white and red canvas tents that were at least three metres tall, I wasn't expecting them to be that big. But I didn't see many soldiers thankfully.

Just in case, I placed my hands on the cold hilts of my swords to be on the safe side, as I continued to walk through the main camp I smelt warming hints of thick smoke and warn spices. Reminding me of the tastes of wild boar cooking over the flesh of some enemies I had years ago. That was a great night. (The guy made it even better)

Listening to the crackling of flames and distant talking of soldiers, I knew I wasn't alone but I never intended it to be. I was actually hoping this place would be crawling with ugly soldiers so I would have a worthy fight.

I stared ahead as I clocked the main tent tens of metres away, my eyes narrowed on its massive size as I focused on it. The size never truly bothered me but there being only one entrance, that did bother me.

A part of me wondered what if I slice into the canvas on the sides and walk in that way, but I forced that idea away as I realised that presented me with too many problems and unknowns.

Perhaps the only thing I hated more than the Overlord (my idiot of a father) was unknowns, in my line of work they were far, far too dangerous.

Which is another reason why I wanted to make sure this military camp was annihilated, with the camp destroyed the enemy wouldn't be able to ride back to the Overlord and by the time news of the mission had failed reached the Overlord, the rebels would have already moved their operations.

So I had, I absolutely had to find where they kept the explosives.

Out of the corner of my eye I noticed two black armoured guards walking towards me, they weren't looking at me but I knew the closer they got the more chance of them looking, and finding me suspicious,

If I was an amateur (which I am nowhere near) I probably would have changed course or run away, but that's so sloppy and to no surprise to me those assassins died far too quickly.

As I'm a professional I simply kept walking, standing straight and projecting my right to be here.

The guards passed and they saluted me, which I was a bit surprised at but if they want to salute the person who will ultimately hack them to pieces, more power to them.

Knowing I was getting closer to the main tent, I noted there was a crossroads of sorts up ahead and I rolled my eyes when I saw three squads of warriors marching towards the main tent. If that wasn't bad enough, I saw three Captains salute me.

What was with these people and saluting me!

Knowing I had to keep walking towards the main tent, I took a deep smoky breath and projected my confidence as I walked.

When I got in front of the main tent I slid into a squad as all three of them stood at attention outside. A small part of me wanted to whip out my swords and slaughter them all. I could easily kill most of them before they even reacted, but I had to behave.

The idea of behaving myself and not killing these horrific fools was very hard as every breath smelled of sweat, blood and rotten flesh. I wouldn't be surprised if one of these idiots had gangrene fever.

I smiled a little as I thought about offering them help with their condition by slicing off their arms and legs. That I could easily do.

The sound of rustling canvas made me look back

at the main tent as I noticed a large muscular man in heavy ornate armour march out. I suppose he's meant to be in charge. I frowned as four guards in thick golden armour joined him, they thrusted their staffs into the ground.

I like a challenge.

As much as I knew I shouldn't have been surprised at the Overlord not being here but my blood still boiled at that. I wanted to rip his throat out or ripped his guts out and make him watch.

"You all have new orders. I received a bird from our traitor. The tunnels will be secured for us shortly. Your mission is to storm them. Long Live The Overlord," the Ornate Armoured man said.

"Long Live The Overlord!" everyone said.

With everyone starting to move, I subtly moved myself to the back of the three squads as they marched towards their horses.

My mind spun a little at the idea of the traitor allowing the enemy to kill all the rebels, but what I was really horrified at was how stupid the traitor was. Did they really, really believe the Overlord wouldn't kill them afterwards?

I checked behind me to see the ornate armoured man and his guards had gotten back into the main tent, no one else was watching the main tent or me.

Sliding away I crouched into the rows upon rows of white and red canvas tents as I sneaked up to the main tent.

When I was there I found a little gap in the main

tent and I smiled as I saw the guards and the ornate armoured man left the tent once again.

Taking out my sword I sliced open the canvas and stepped inside.

I had to find something useful here. I had to find those explosives. Or at the very least I had to chop off the ornate armoured man's head.

Cut off the head and the body dies.

CHAPTER 18

Commander Coleman hated what was happening to his rebellion, he hated to think what his father would have thought about him. Coleman knew his father would never call him a failure but if his father wasn't disappointed with him then Coleman would have wondered what was wrong with his father.

Inside the dark cave tunnel with its smooth yellow curved walls, Coleman stood close to the heavy wooden door and hoped it would hold. But as he heard the enemy slam into it, shouting and screaming bloody murder outside.

He didn't know how much longer the door would last.

The sound thundered down the cave tunnel. Coleman hated all of this so he gripped the warm hilt of his sword and raised it.

If the enemy didn't storm in then Coleman was going to kill them.

The smell of fearful, cold sweat (that reminded

him of salty bacon) filled the tunnel as Coleman heard the mutters and shivering of his friends. They were all losing hope, they were all going to die, they were all going to blame Coleman.

Coleman didn't want to believe them but they were right, he had failed them all. His so-called master plans were failing one by one.

Looking around Coleman hoped, he really hoped this next stage wouldn't fail because if it did then there was only one place left to make a final stand. Coleman wouldn't allow these bastards to take his home.

This was his cause, his family, his life. The enemy were not taking it from him.

The sounds of slamming and shouting stopped for a moment. Coleman leant forward and pressed his ear against the heavy cold wood.

It sounded like the enemy were walking away and laughing. They were laughing! Cocking his head Coleman tried to understand why but he had no idea why the enemy would stop.

Rebels screamed.

Heads were smashed.

Necks were snapped.

Bodies were hacked apart.

Coleman looked at the door.

It was intact.

The enemy didn't come in.

The wall exploded.

Throwing Coleman into the air.

He slammed into the wall.
His ears rang.
Black armoured soldiers stormed out.
The tunnels!
The enemy must have dug through the tunnels.
Soldiers poured out.
Coleman jumped up.
His ears still rang.
A soldier grabbed Coleman.
Whacking him across the face.
The soldier picked him up by the throat.
Throwing him against the wall.
Coleman looked nearby.
Soldiers were stabbing Rebels.
Their knifes moving too quick to escape.
His hearing returned.
The hand around his throat squeezed.
Screaming filled the air.
The door exploded.
Shattering the wood.
Sending lethal shards into the rebels and enemy.
Coleman dropped.
The soldier's corpse on the ground.
Coleman whipped out his sword.
He charged.
The enemy poured in.
Coleman swung.
Slicing into flesh.
Slicing into armour.
Blood sprayed everywhere.

Covering Coleman's chest.
He smiled.
The enemy slaughtered the rebels.
The enemy didn't care.
Their swords chomped on their flesh.
Ripping it out.
Coleman fell back.
He swung his sword.
Again and again.
He kicked them.
Shattering their skulls.
Slicing into their chests.
Ripping open their throats.
Corpses fell.
It was useless.
This was utter slaughter.
The enemy advanced up the tunnel.
Pushing the Rebels back further.
Massacring the Rebels more.
Rebels died every second.
Coleman screamed in defiance.
He wasn't losing!
He charged forward.
Diving into the enemy swarm.
He swung.
In a bloody arc.
Again and again.
Corpses dropped.
Blood splashed up armour.
A fist slammed into him.

Coleman fell to the ground.

His vision blurred.

Fear gripped him.

Laughter filled the air.

He saw swords move.

Coleman tried to move.

He was too weak.

His vision twisted.

Hands grabbed him.

Screams of agony filled his ears.

Coleman let the hands take him.

He saw shadow after shadow jump over him.

His vision cleared.

Rebels flew at the enemy.

Swords hacked them apart.

Coleman jumped up.

He had to go.

It was time for a final stand.

CHAPTER 19

I silently stepped into the massive white and red canvas tent, my hands firmly on the warm hilts of my swords. If the enemy wanted to attack me, they were going to die.

Taking a shallow breath of the smoke filled air that reminded me of smoked apples over a roaring fire with my friends years ago, my eyes narrowed as I studied the main tent, there had to be something here.

In all my years of experience (and killing), everything precious to the enemy is always kept here. You just need to know how to find it.

Listening to the crackling of fire and quiet chatting of the guards outside, I rolled my eyes at the simplicity of the tent, I would have expected there to be golden decorates, grand icons of the foul Overlord and more horrors. But no.

For the tent's massive size the white and red canvas walls were plain and unloved with the only thing of note being a large brown desk with piles of documents on it. But I did like the large wooden crates nearby.

As I silently walked over to the desk, with a flickering candle on there, my eyes were fixed on the opening in the tent, which I presumed was the door, if I had known the desk was in direct line of sight from outside. I would have grabbed a bow and shot the ornate armour man in the head.

Running my fingers over the cold smooth wooden desk, I flicked through the piles of documents and I had no idea how many battle orders it took to get an army. Actually what I couldn't believe the amount of documents needed for the army to pass checkpoints every ten miles.

I rolled my eyes at the idea of the Overlord's security tightening, I didn't need to kill more soldiers just so I could move City to City. Well, I didn't need to but I wanted to, so it would hardly be a problem.

Knowing guards would back any minute, I pulled my long black leather trench coat and black hood over myself tightly. A part of me was hoping if an enemy walked passed they would think I was just another regular soldier in black armour. A bit insulting but that was my plan.

Turning my attention to the large wooden crates nearby, I ran my fingers over the rough wood and smiled as I popped one open.

My eyes widened and my smile deepened as I saw crates upon crates of black powder. My mind tried to understand how a military camp could have so much in one place.

It was like they were asking to be annihilated, and it's rude not to do what people ask!

My smile lessened when I looked at the large drag marks on the ground where other crates had been. I swore under my breath at the thought of the Rebels being exploded and ripped to shreds.

As much as I wanted to play here and let my blades swirl and twirl into the flesh of my enemy, I knew I had to go. I had to save them.

We all underestimated the Overlord and what he wanted.

I wanted to kick myself for this, if I had been better or worked harder or... I took a deep smoky breath as I remembered I was still here fighting for the Rebellion. I hadn't failed yet, the Rebels were bound to be alive, I just had to help them.

Picking up the flickering candle on the desk, I looked at the opened crate of gunpowder. This was crazy. This was wrong. I didn't even know how long I would have to escape.

Just to be on the safe(r) side, I walked over to the door, the flickering candle burning in my hand.

I heard the ornate armoured man coming.

His guards were charging.

I looked at the crate.

I looked at the candle.

What the heck?

I threw it.

The flame touched the candle.

I ran.
I RAN!
My feet pounded into the ground.
Guards flew at me.
Guards swung at me.
I jumped into the air.
I wasn't fighting.
I was running.
I whistled.
The main tent burned.
The guards shouted.
They moaned.
They threw things.
Arrows flew through the air.
I whistled again.
A guard tackled me.
My head hitting the ground.
This wasn't happening!
I grabbed his head.
Snapping his neck.
I jumped up.
I charged.
The black powder exploded.
Only one crate.
Flaming chunks of canvas rained down.
Engulfing more tents.
Guards screamed in rage.
More arrows flew at me.
I felt the flames lick my coat.
A horse passed me.

I jumped on.
The other crates exploded.
I kicked my horse.
It zoomed away.
The military camp was annihilated.
Now I had to save the Rebels.

CHAPTER 20

Commander Coleman felt drop after drop of cold fearful sweat pour off his forehead, he really hated how much of a failure he had become.

He looked around the Inner Keep, the most secure and innermost chamber in the Rebel base, he normally loved looking at its smooth dome yellow walls and those amazing little detailed carvings of warriors.

Coleman hated all of it all today, especially when as he looked into the cold wide eyes of the last hundred Rebels with their pale skin.

Breathing in the sweat filled air, Coleman wished he could comfort them but he couldn't even comfort himself. There was no hope.

The enemy had taken over the base and they were the final members of the Rebellion. The only hope for an entire nation, but they were all going to die. Coleman knew that, he just didn't want to admit it.

As he listened to mutters and talks of surrender, Coleman wanted to jump up and tell his people why they shouldn't surrender why he couldn't. He didn't have the energy or the conviction.

Maybe if he did surrender the Overlord would enslave his friends and work them to death. But at least his friends would be alive.

Coleman smiled as he remembered the Assassin's beautiful face and that amazing long black leather trench coat and that black hood, he loved it. Coleman hadn't seen a more beautiful woman in his life.

Shaking his head Coleman knew he wouldn't surrender, she would never forgive him for starts. And the idea of stunning Jasmine thinking less of Coleman made him frown and hate himself. How dare he even consider surrender and enslavement.

The sounds of thumping and slamming came from the thick red wooden door ahead of Coleman. He knew it would hold a lot longer than the last one but after this… it was do or die.

There was nowhere else to run or hide. If Coleman died here then he would be happy. Coleman smiled at the idea of being a martyr for the cause, a martyr for freedom, a martyr for a Kingdom with people being forced into a specific path in life.

Standing up, Coleman whipped out his sword and checked his dagger was still in his pocket. He wasn't going to give up. He smiled as he heard every other Rebel stand up and take out their weapons.

"We fight!" Coleman shouted.

"Death to the Overlord," everyone returned.

Coleman was about to say something when he felt an icy cold blade press against his throat.

A part of him thought if it was the Assassin but he knew it wouldn't be.

"Sis, what ya doing?" Abbic asked.

Coleman's eyes widened as he realised Barbic was the traitor all along. He wanted to channel his inner assassin but that wasn't going to happen. Not with a blade at his throat.

"Traitor. How long? Why do it?" Coleman asked.

Barbic moved Coleman closed to the door. "Three years to help my father,"

Coleman wanted to cock his head but the blade made it difficult.

"The Overlord ya father Sis. Can't be. Daddy's-"

"You always were stupid Abbic. I am not your sister, your mother and father adopted me you stupid girl,"

"Why Abbic's family?" Coleman asked.

"Because they were friends with your father. Now you will all die and the Rebellion will end,"

"Sis ya don't want this!"

The blade pressed harder against Coleman's throat.

"I am not your sister! I will kill him right now! Back off!"

Coleman held out his hand to tell his friends he was going to be okay. As much as his heart thumped in his chest he knew he had to buy the Assassin time to arrive.

"Your father will die,"

"Coleman, yes he will. I will kill him when the time is right, but you will die first,"

"Why kill your own father?"

"He is foul, dirt. I will rule the Kingdom,"

"You won't be better than him,"

"I will be. My Father is soft on these commoners,"

"Your father kills thousands each day,"

"Thousands must die. They must be tortured. Complete obedience must happen,"

Coleman rolled his eyes. Barbic was a great actor but Coleman knew she had lost the plot. She needed to die.

"I presume you want us to open the door and let your friends inside," Coleman asked.

"Of course idiot. Your Rebels friends will be enslaved and turned into mindless drones for the glorious Overlord!"

As much as Coleman hated that idea he had a feeling (A gut feeling? He didn't know) that the Assassin was close.

"What will happen to me?"

The blade cut slightly into his throat. Coleman gagged.

"You Traitor rebel, you will be sent to the Overlord and killed in the capital. All those glorious people must see the glory of their God,"

Coleman's eyes narrowed. He didn't know the

Capital people saw the Overlord as a god. Interesting.

"Open it!" Barbic shouted.

She forced Coleman over to the door and Coleman slowly opened it. The door creaked open and men hissed as they pulled it open from the other side.

Coleman felt his stomach twist into a tight knot as he saw tens upon tens of large black armoured warriors, their long swords shining with the dark rich blood of his friends.

The smell of the blood was overpowering and disgusting, Coleman hated this but he had what he wanted.

Coleman grabbed his pocket.

He whipped out a dagger.

Thrusting it into Barbic's leg.

She hissed.

The blade fell away.

He ripped out the dagger.

Coleman spun.

Thrusting it into her chest.

Again and again.

Blood poured out.

Coleman grabbed her head.

Pulling it back.

Exposing her throat.

He ripped into it.

Blood gushed out.

Covering him.

Coleman spun to the warriors.

They froze.

A warrior screamed.

Coleman looked at the cave entrance.

A woman was here.

Slashing and lashing.

Her long black leather trench coat flapping about.

Coleman smiled.

He charged.

This was now do or die.

A final stand.

A fight for survival.

CHAPTER 21

Utter lust filled me as I stepped into the cave entrance of the rebel base. I loved the beautiful splashes of wet dripping blood on the smooth rocky walls of the cave. This was going to be great!

Walking inside my smile deepened as I smelt the vapourised blood and the desperation in the air. It was cross between a fearful sweat and another smell I couldn't quite describe.

I admired the lumps and bumps on the rough cave floor as I kept walking, occasionally having to step over skulls and shattered bodies.

All this death and destruction was perfect, as an assassin this was wonderous for me. The sound of shouting and taunting in the distance echoed around the cave.

A small part of me hated the arrogance of those foul black armoured soldiers ahead. I hated them, everyone hated them.

But I couldn't be too mad at them, after all they

were kind enough to make themselves trapped so I can slaughter them all. My stomach filled with butterflies at the idea of ripping into their amazing flesh.

An assassin's dream.

To make sure nothing caught on any random rocks or edges, I pulled my long black leather trench coat and hood tight over me. Nothing was going to stop me doing this.

Taking a final few steps forward, I whipped out my swords and smiled at all the black armoured sacks of flesh and blood that were completely blind to my presence.

The sound of the heavy wooden door opening and the soldiers' laughter made me cock my head. What were the stupid rebels doing?

My eyes narrowed as I saw that Barbic woman was the traitor. Typical. I knew Coleman with those amazing emerald eyes needed a distraction. Who was I to refuse?

I charged.

Ramming my sword into a soldier.

He screamed.

Coleman killed Barbic.

Wonderful man.

I threw the corpse to the ground.

More guards moved.

They were too slow.

I flew at them.

My sword swirling in the air.

Slicing into their flesh.
Blood poured out.
Painting the ground red.
I smiled.
I charged.
Soldiers were alert.
They swung.
They ducked.
I slid on the ground.
Sliding forward.
Thrusting up my swords.
Slicing in between their legs.
Blood flooded out.
Corpses dropped.
I jumped up.
Arrows flew at me.
I dodged.
I saw archers.
They reloaded.
Too slow.
I charged.
Jumping into the air.
Landing on them.
Wrapping my legs around her neck.
I swung my weight.
Throwing her forward.
She smashed into the wall.
Cracking her skull open.
I landed.
Thrusting my swords into the archers.

Their bodies went limp.
Bodies littered the ground.
Rebels poured out.
Hacking the enemy to pieces.
Ripping into their flesh.
Fists slammed into me.
My head whacked the wall.
Blood splashed up it.
More fists whacked me.
I dropped my swords.
My nose cracked.
Someone grabbed my head.
Ripping off my hood.
Grabbing my hair.
No more.
I backflipped.
Ripping out my hair.
I landed.
Wrapping my legs around their neck.
Grabbing their face.
Pressing my fingers into their eyes.
They screamed.
I pressed harder.
Blood squirted out.
My fingers wet and warm.
The corpse dropped.
I picked up my swords.
More foes ahead.
Slicing through the Rebels.
Coleman staggered.

He was hurt.
Blood dripped from his stomach.
I had to help him.
Five soldiers surrounded him.
Rage filled me.
No one hurts Coleman.
I roared.
I flew.
The enemy turned.
It didn't matter.
I swung my swords.
Swords ripping into flesh.
Two dead.
A male slapped me.
He slapped me again.
I chopped off his hand.
He screamed.
I grabbed his cut-off hand.
Throwing it at him.
He screamed.
I dashed over.
Snapping his neck.
Three dead.
The last two fired arrows.
I jumped.
I landed.
I dropped to the ground.
Kicking them.
Knocking their feet out from under them.
They fell.

I leapt up.

Slashing their throats.

As I slowly got up I noticed rebel after rebel, in all their shapes and sizes with different amounts of blood covering them, run past me but I simply stood there amongst all the corpses.

The battle was won.

I turned to my beautiful Coleman he was alive and in that moment that's all I cared about, sure I knew there were other traitors in the base, but the other rebels could kill them.

I... I just wanted to make sure my Coleman was okay, because without him there was no rebellion, no hope, no nothing, and for me without him there was no... joy.

I needed him.

CHAPTER 22

Commander Coleman smiled as he stood firm, looking out over the amazing, stunning valley below him with the black dagger-like mountain range lining the edges of the valley. It was all so beautiful, so amazing, Coleman didn't want to lose it.

But times change.

Breathing in the sweet piney air of the mountains, Coleman embraced the cold chill as he savoured it and studied every little beautiful detail of the mountain range and valley.

Even now Coleman wasn't sure what his favourite part of the valley was, but he loved it all. He knew that, especially the little rabbits and deer running around on the valley ground.

As he listened to the cold air gently howl and the distance talking of rebels, Coleman knew he had done well today. He never ever expected today to be successful, he actually expected to die today.

Coleman gave a half smile as he wondered about the idea of dying as a martyr. A small part of him loved the idea of dying as a symbol of hope, justice and unity. A person who died so others may live in peace, that is what Coleman wanted to die for.

Feeling the soft fabric and bandages tied tightly around his stomach, Coleman brushed his fingers over the soft material. It was a reminder that anyone could die and that his days were numbered.

Coleman didn't have a problem with this, he loved the idea of it, but he had to complete his mission first, one day at a time.

As much as Coleman wanted today never to happen, he was proud of himself and his rebels. They were the real heroes, they were fighters who died, sacrificed and made sure the Rebellion fought another day.

Breathing in more of the refreshing piney air, Coleman nodded to himself as he realised that he had done right today. He had made sure people could live in peace and make their own choices in life.

His amazing, beautiful rebels had chosen to stay and fight for him, for the cause, for each other, and he rewarded them by fighting to make sure they could live in peace when it was all over.

Coleman smiled at that realisation, he hadn't thought of it like that before, he had always considered today to be a failure.

And it was.

Looking over the edge of the high mountain top he stood on, Coleman frowned as he saw the hundreds upon hundreds of rebel corpses that littered the ground and turned the black rock red.

None of this should have happened, that was a fact, but for Coleman there was a little bit of hope attached to the failure. Coleman noticed thousands of more Overlord corpses compared to the Rebels.

They had won.

Coleman shook his head about all the killing and executions him and the beautiful Jasmine had to do after the battle. There were so many traitors within their ranks that had to die, even more Overlord soldiers that were hiding in the corners of the base. They all had to die.

It was still a victory. The Rebellion was alive.

And that's what Coleman smiled about, he knew the next few months would be a nightmare, trying to find a new base and set up everyone, then try and find new rebels. It would be a challenge.

Coleman's eyes widened at the challenge, he loved it, a challenge is probably what kept him going. He wasn't fighting the Overlord because it was easy, he was fighting because he wanted people to live in peace and choose their own lives.

There's nothing easy about that!

Coleman wiped his soft cheeks with his rough hands as he remembered killing his friend, Barbic. The entire thing about her being a traitor was so… ridiculous but it had happened.

He didn't know how it happened, how he could let a traitor into their ranks but it wasn't the first, it wouldn't be the last, Coleman just had to be ready. He hoped a certain special Assassin would help him, but he wasn't sure.

Knowing there was a lot of planning to do and it was going to be interesting to get the Rebels ready to move, Coleman started to turn around.

As he looked at the piles of corpses and his Rebels picking through the bodies, taking armour and weapons (Coleman hated the necessary evil), Coleman saw a beautiful woman in her amazing long black leather trench coat and a little black hood.

If someone had asked him if the Assassin would have ever saved them before today, Coleman would have tried to deny it but he ultimately would have said no. He had no idea the Assassin even cared about the Rebellion, Coleman always thought it was the coin that kept her coming back.

It wasn't.

That fact was still mind blowing to Coleman, he didn't understand it, he loved her but she didn't love him. So why keep coming back?

Coleman smiled at the idea of the Assassin secretly liking him and just being too scared to admit it. He shook those thoughts away when he remembered how well she fought and killed. Jasmine wasn't afraid of anything.

Starting to walk down to the corpses below, Coleman just smiled at everything, him and his Rebellion were alive and thankfully so was Jasmine. That's all he wanted.

A part of him wondered if Jasmine would stay now the Rebellion was safe or if she would go again and make sure she was just another assassin, killing for coin and nothing more.

Coleman hoped not, he needed her. He was just afraid to ask.

As his mother used to say, don't ask questions, you don't want the answer to.

CHAPTER 23

Looking at a stunning corpse in front of me, I loved the way how the blood had pooled in the little cracks in the rocks, creating wonderfully dark rich blood pools.

Standing up, I stretched my back and smiled as I saw the thousands of enemy and Rebel corpses around me. I still love the massive streaks of dried blood on the black rocky slopes of the mountain. It was a great sight.

I didn't even care about the blood stains on my long black leather trench coat and I hoped no one was going to ask how I got blood on my black hood.

I took a deep bitter piney breath and licked my lips at the hints of vapourised blood in the air, this was a battle and a half. So many lives lost and so many corpses on the ground.

The damn Rebellion and them giving me a conscience felt a little sad at the sight, I normally never would have felt like this after a battle, but I did.

The idea of so many lives lost was staggering, that's why my father had to die. All those lives ruined and lives lost for his stupid ambitions.

Listening to the Rebels cry, talk and pull armour and weapons off the dead, I rolled my eyes as I wished they would stop crying. People were always going to die today but I hope, I really hope I lessened that number.

Feeling the cold mountain air wash over me, I cast my mind back to why I did all of this, I wanted to keep the Rebellion alive and protect that stunning Commander Coleman.

I had to smile as I stared at all the slaughtered, hacked up bodies of the enemy. Their corpses dripping blood and the Rebels walking around me, that made me smile.

Before today I would have smiled for the sole reason that there was lots and lots of beautiful blood on the ground (of course I still smile at that), but I smiled because my friends were alive too.

That's what the rebellion are to me, they aren't people who give me coins and I kill for them, they are people who love me, respect my work and want me for me. Most of them don't see a living weapon to use like a pet, they see me as a person.

So if someone asks me if I'm pleased that I saved them, I am. I really am. Now I have friends, a family and a hope for getting revenge.

I'm still not sure if that's what I want, I want (or think I do) Coleman, his beautiful body, face and those amazing emerald eyes. I might want him in the future but I don't want him just yet. I can't become involved with him in my state, I'm a killer, a cold calculating killer, I'm not made for relationships.

But I'll be lying if I said seeing him bleeding and hurt wasn't troubling, I wanted to lash out and kill everyone, ram by swords into every one, I had to protect him, and that's what I wanted to continue. No one hurts my Coleman, no matter how much I hate to admit it.

Taking another look around, I saw a group of Rebels laughing and smiling, truly smiling, they were having fun and enjoying life. That… made me feel something, pride? Joy? I don't know but I want more of that feeling, the feeling of what I do matters and it makes a difference.

For almost my entire life I've been taught to kill and do it for money and food and for survival, but now I want something different, I want a life worth living.

And because of that damn Rebellion with their kind words, warm hearts and their cause, I want them to succeed, I want them to kill the Overlord and free the Kingdom.

Smiling to myself I knew that was impossible without me, even I have to admit the Rebels were better than I thought, but I've killed, I've fought too many of the Overlord's soldiers to know the Rebels won't win. They don't have the armour, weapons or tactical intelligence to know how to beat the

Overlord.

So I will be with them for a little while, I'll fight and I'll protect them. Oh, I might be able to get a special title with that mission in mind, I like the sound of that.

Damn the Rebellion!

Knowing I was truly changing because of these people and their cause, I gave a little chuckle to myself at the oddity of it all. I never expected to be like this or have anything close to friends.

As I looked at the tall amazing man walking towards me with that smooth squarish face and those amazing green emerald eyes, I knew I was wrong, very wrong.

Walking over to handsome Coleman, I knew I had to help him move all the Rebels, find a new base and most importantly help them fight the Overlord and free the Kingdom.

Coleman gave me a stunning smile that made me want to hug him, and as I looked into those deep emerald eyes. I felt something special towards him, after all Coleman was one of the few living people who knew my name. A very dangerous thing, a thing of trust too.

Taking a step closer to him, I loved the feeling of his body warmth on my skin.

"I'll stay with you. I'll help you fight. But I need something in return," I said.

A small part of me wanted to say him so badly, I think I really wanted him in that moment, but I couldn't say it just yet.

"What?" he asked, smiling.

I hope he wasn't expecting me to say him too.

"I want to be known as the Protectorate of the Rebellion, Swore Protector and all that,"

To my surprise, Coleman smiled and I thought he was going to laugh.

"Sure, my Lord Protectorate,"

I don't know why but having my own little title made me feel special and important, something I've never felt before, I've never truly mattered to anyone, but things were changing.

I was about to start walking but Coleman gently grabbed my shoulder and smiled at me.

"Barbic, she said something that I didn't like?"

I smiled. "What?"

"She said the Overlord was her Father. Making her your-"

"Sister or half-sister," I said, slowly. I had no idea about a sister, it was always just me and my little perfect brother before…he died.

I just nodded. There was nothing I could say to that. I hated the idea of having other family out there but after seeing the treachery Barbic had committed, I wasn't sure I wanted to meet these other family members.

"What ever happened to those Hunters I thought they'll be here?" Coleman asked.

I cocked my head and thought for a moment.

"We didn't see them after the Overlord trapped

us so I fear I was right all along. The Overlord was after me, he sent the Hunters to hunt me and that's it,"

"Think they'll return,"

I smiled at that and placed my hands on the hilts of my swords.

"I hope so,"

He nodded at that.

As me and Coleman walked over to the Rebel base to finish the move before we headed out, I knew fighting the Overlord, Hunters and my family were all tomorrow's problems, and I had found my true family, not of blood but of friendship (or something very close to that).

A family I was going to protect to the end.

AUTHOR'S NOTE

I really hope you enjoyed that story, I know for me I had a blast writing it.

The entire story behind the story was really strange for me and it was a first. Because I've done City of Assassins short stories for a little while.

The first one (*City of Fire*) was done in January 2021 as an assignment on a writing course I was doing, then the second one (Awaiting Death) was a story I wrote after my Great Uncle died in March 2021.

Then I let the series until August 2021 and I was writing along then I got to the end of City of Vengeance (I really encourage you to read it) and I realised there was a massive event coming.

No short story was going to cover the invasion of the rebel base, so I decided to write a novella. And before you ask there will definitely be a series out of this because I really want to know:

- How will the Rebels defeat the Overlord?

- Will the Assassin kill her father?
- Will Coleman and the Assassin ever get together?

But I'm also interested in how will the Assassin change over the course of the series. Because from the beginning of the book to the end, there's a lot of change in her and we learn a lot more about her.

This will be interesting!

So I really hoped you enjoyed this little behind the scenes Author's Note and I look forward to seeing you in another book.

Have a great day!

GET YOUR FREE AND EXCLUSIVE SHORT STORY NOW! LEARN ABOUT NEMESIO'S PAST!

https://www.subscribepage.com/fireheart

About the author:

Connor Whiteley is the author of over 60 books in the sci-fi fantasy, nonfiction psychology and books for writer's genre and he is a Human Branding Speaker and Consultant.

He is a passionate warhammer 40,000 reader, psychology student and author.

Who narrates his own audiobooks and he hosts The Psychology World Podcast.

All whilst studying Psychology at the University of Kent, England.

Also, he was a former Explorer Scout where he gave a speech to the Maltese President in August 2018 and he attended Prince Charles' 70th Birthday Party at Buckingham Palace in May 2018.

Plus, he is a self-confessed coffee lover!

OTHER SHORT STORIES BY CONNOR WHITELEY

Blade of The Emperor
Arbiter's Truth
The Bloodied Rose
Asmodia's Wrath
Heart of A Killer
Emissary of Blood
Computation of Battle
Old One's Wrath
Puppets and Masters
Ship of Plague
Interrogation
Sacrifice of the Soul
Heart of The Flesheater
Heart of The Regent
Heart of The Standing
Feline of The Lost
Heart of The Story
The Family Mailing Affair
Defining Criminality
The Martian Affair
A Cheating Affair
The Little Café Affair
Mountain of Death
Prisoner's Fight
Claws of Death

Bitter Air
Honey Hunt
Blade On A Train
City of Fire
Awaiting Death
Poison In The Candy Cane
Christmas Innocence
You Better Watch Out
Christmas Theft
Trouble In Christmas
Smell of The Lake
Problem In A Car
Theft, Past and Team

Other books by Connor Whiteley:
The Fireheart Fantasy Series
Heart of Fire
Heart of Lies
Heart of Prophecy
Heart of Bones
Heart of Fate

City of Assassins (Urban Fantasy)
City of Death

Agents of The Emperor
Return of The Ancient Ones

The Garro Series- Fantasy/Sci-fi
GARRO: GALAXY'S END
GARRO: RISE OF THE ORDER
GARRO: END TIMES
GARRO: SHORT STORIES
GARRO: COLLECTION
GARRO: HERESY
GARRO: FAITHLESS
GARRO: DESTROYER OF WORLDS
GARRO: COLLECTIONS BOOK 4-6
GARRO: MISTRESS OF BLOOD
GARRO: BEACON OF HOPE
GARRO: END OF DAYS

Winter Series- Fantasy Trilogy Books
WINTER'S COMING
WINTER'S HUNT
WINTER'S REVENGE
WINTER'S DISSENSION

Miscellaneous:
RETURN
FREEDOM
SALVATION

www.ingramcontent.com/pod-product-compliance
Lightning Source LLC
LaVergne TN
LVHW011838060526
838200LV00053B/4082